CRASH
DIVE

BY CRAIG DILOUIE

CRASH

DIVE

A NOVEL OF THE PACIFIC WAR

CRAIG DILOUIE

CRASH DIVE
A novel of the Pacific War
©2015 Craig DiLouie. All rights reserved.

Cover art by Eloise Knapp Design.

Published by ZING Communications, Inc.

www.CraigDiLouie.com

FOREWORD

BY JOHN DIXON

I'm a Craig DiLouie fan. Like so many others, I came for the zombies and stayed for the characters, tension, and high-quality writing. Then, in 2015, his Bram Stoker Award-nominated *Suffer the Children* chiseled the name Craig DiLouie onto a short list of my favorite writers.

All this being said, I approached his WWII submarine adventures with a degree of uncertainty. As a long-time fan of both the Horatio Hornblower series and the Aubrey / Maturin books, I was dubious.

How wrong I was to worry.

Fans of DiLouie's horror novels will in the *Crash Dive* series quickly recognize the dynamic characters, volatile relationships, and ever-burgeoning tension that made them fall in love with his horror novels. If you've enjoyed Craig DiLouie in the past, you are going to love these books.

If you're new to Craig DiLouie, I envy you. I really do. You're in for one hell of a ride.

DiLouie isn't a Michener or a Clancy. Unlike these authors' fat thrillers — which always strike me as novels trick-or-treating as creative nonfiction — DiLouie's adventure stories are as fast and sleek and explosive as torpedoes.

DiLouie has clearly done his research but has internalized that knowledge, bringing it forth compactly, providing verisimilitude through a strong sense of place and procedure without slowing the story... ever. The writing is as masculine and stripped down as the subs themselves. The result is a first-rate adventure as relentlessly character- and story-driven as the pulps of the early twentieth century but without their unrealistic protagonists and sometimes purple prose.

Charlie Harrison is a great character, one part chess player, one part street fighter, a man whose greatest asset and liability are one in the same: his irrepressibly aggressive nature. He's very human: tough and likeable and self-sacrificing, a man who makes mistakes but never freezes during a crisis, even when it means putting his own life— and the lives of those who serve alongside him—on the line.

When we first meet Charlie, he's a junior officer just beginning his virgin posting on a combat submarine, much like Horatio Hornblower in *Mr. Midshipman Hornblower*. Charlie faces a daunting task to say the least: cooperate with an often antagonistic crew—banging heads with both the enlisted men and his fellow officers—to wage war against the Imperial Japanese Navy... all while trapped in a cramped and leaking submarine that sometimes feels less like a ship of a line and more like an armed coffin.

For readers, these primitive submarines and their limitations provide part of the fun and a good portion of the terror. The submarines we see in the *Crash Dive* series have more in common with World War I biplanes than with the hyper-modern nuclear subs of today's navy. The subs are ancient, battered, and fraught with potentially fatal problems.

There are so many ways to die. Depth charges, machine guns, bombs dropped from planes; they can be boarded by the Japanese ... on the surface; fires, poison gasses, disease; drown... always the threat of the malfunctioning submarine sinking to the bottom and taking them with it.

To survive, Charlie and his crewmates must be smart and sly, resourceful and vigilant, tough and tireless, much like the men and women of the Greatest Generation upon whom they are based. Crammed together, inflamed by disagreements, they must nonetheless work together to defeat the enemy and stay alive... two goals sometimes very much at odds. Simply to attack, they must expose themselves to discovery and all that follows: deck guns, airplanes, and the dreaded depth charges. But the men forge ahead, working in close quarters under extreme pressure, with death never farther away than the thickness of the hull. The stench of their unwashed bodies blends with the smells of the ship, creating an olfactory swamp of sweat and blood and diesel, as the submariners meld with the ship itself, flesh-and-blood cogs in a terrible war machine. Uniform codes wick away, and beards spring forth as the men sweat and stink and swear... until, at last, the submarine more closely resembles a raiding pirate ship than something we might expect to find in any modern navy.

This is adventure in the grand tradition: high stakes on

the high seas, gripping stories that move at frenetic pace without sacrificing character or detail. I read both in two sittings, literally on the edge of my seat. They are short not because they've left something out but because they've included nothing extra. As a result, *Crash Dive* pounds relentlessly forward, locked unwaveringly on their target: excellent storytelling.

Batten down the hatches, damn the torpedoes, and dive, dive, dive!

—John Dixon
Author of *Phoenix Island*

AREA OF OPERATIONS.
THE GUADALCANAL CAMPAIGN.

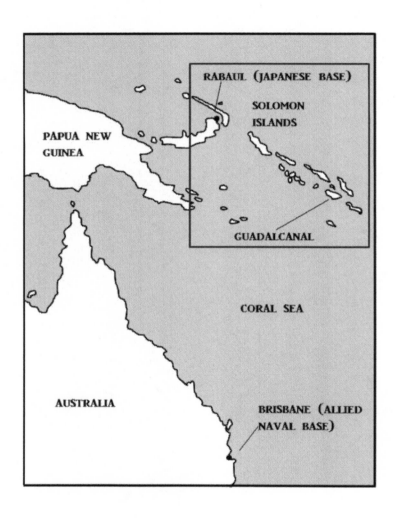

RABAUL (JAPANESE BASE)

SOLOMON
ISLANDS

PAPUA NEW
GUINEA

GUADALCANAL

CORAL SEA

AUSTRALIA

BRISBANE (ALLIED
NAVAL BASE)

CHAPTER ONE
TO WAR

Brisbane, Australia.

October, 1942.

Charlie Harrison was going to war.

He walked onto the busy New Farm Wharf, sea bag over his shoulder and a spring in his step. He fidgeted, six feet of coiled energy. Then he shook it off, determined to appear cool in case anybody was watching.

He'd worked hard to get here. Naval Academy, class of '40. He'd served as a lieutenant, junior-grade on a destroyer, steaming up and down the Atlantic for two years. After the Japanese surprise attack against Pearl electrified America, he'd put in for a transfer.

He didn't want to spend the war playing cat and mouse with German U-boats. He didn't want to play defense; he wanted to take the fight to the enemy.

The Navy approved his transfer, and he attended the Submarine School at New London in Connecticut.

Now he stood on the eastern coast of Australia, ready to report to his new command.

He found the S-55 tied to a tender, a big repair and

support ship. Men labored among an assortment of hoses, welding lines, and other gear. Welding sprayed showers of sparks into the air. They readied the submarine for sea.

God, but she was ugly. Nothing like the U.S.S. *Kennedy*, his old destroyer with her clean lines, smokestacks, and guns. The S-55 was just a long black cylinder with a short metal sail jutting over her. Built by the Electric Boat Company in 1922, she was one of the last boats of the Great War era.

He'd hoped for love at first sight, but she inspired neither affection nor admiration.

Two hundred twenty feet long and twenty feet wide at the beam. A complement of a dozen torpedoes, which she launched from four tubes in the bow. Forty officers and crew.

She'd seen some heavy fighting. The conning tower wore a patchwork of welded gray plates, scars of some past action.

In that submarine, he'd live ass to elbow in a cramped, dingy, smelly machine for weeks at a time. Not surprisingly, the sailors called them "pigboats." Charlie had trained on an even older R-class submarine at New London and had gotten a taste of it.

He'd heard a depth charge attack felt like being in an earthquake—a quake that could break the hull and send the boat straight to the bottom.

It was a hell of a way to fight a war.

The S-55, his new home, could end up being his coffin. Living in a submarine demanded certain skills and temperament. Those who didn't cut it were put ashore and

2

left there. He wondered if he was as able as he was willing. If he had the right stuff.

Looking at his new home, his romantic ideas about taking the fight to the enemy became real. For the first time, he wondered if he'd made a mistake.

Too late to back out now.

Charlie steeled himself to report to the deck watch, who stood on the gangway with a .45 on his hip. He halted as an apparition in oilskins, gas mask, and thick rubber gloves emerged from the conning tower and descended to the deck. Carrying a metal tank and coiled Flit gun, he stomped down the gangway onto the pier.

He spotted Charlie and lowered his gas mask, revealing the grinning face of a man about the same age. He said, "You wouldn't believe it."

"Believe what?"

"How many cockroaches I just put out of my misery. We're talking millions."

"Did you get Hitler?"

The sailor laughed. "No such luck, brother. You our new junior officer?"

"That's right." Charlie looked up at the scarred metal sail. "When's she going back out on patrol?"

"Last Tuesday. We keep getting delayed with new repairs. This geriatric tub needs a lot of love."

"I'd like you to take me to see the captain then, if you're able."

The man grinned again. "I'll be happy to do that. You got a name, sailor?"

"Lieutenant, j-g Charles Harrison."

"Welcome to the 55, Charlie. I'm Lieutenant Russell Grady, but you can call me Rusty."

Rusty was his senior. Charlie should have saluted. Instead, he'd ordered the man to take him to the captain. He froze, mortified.

Rusty held out his hand. Charlie shook it, grateful for the warm welcome.

He hadn't expected to see an officer doing an enlisted man's duties. His first lesson in submarines. Everybody, officers and crew alike, did their share of the dirty work. On the S-55, as the saying went, they were all in the same boat.

Charlie realized that, despite his schooling, he still had plenty to learn. He also thought, if even half of the crew was like Rusty, he'd feel right at home on the old S-55.

CHAPTER TWO
GOD IS ON OUR SIDE

Rusty whistled up a recreation car. The driver was a matronly Australian woman in a khaki dress uniform who told them her name was Kate Moore. She said her husband was fighting in North Africa, one of the Desert Rats.

She drove them to a rest home that Lieutenant-Commander J.R. Kane, captain of the S-55, had been assigned as his quarters. Rusty explained the captain was hosting a small party.

"What's he like?" Charlie asked.

Rusty stared out the window as Brisbane flashed by. "A cool customer."

"Standoffish, huh?" He'd expected that.

"I mean he's seen a lot of combat, and his hands don't shake."

"The boat looks like it's seen some action."

"That was at Cavite Navy Yard, in the Philippines, when the Japs bombed the Asiatic Fleet."

About ten months ago, the Imperial Japanese Navy staged a stunning surprise attack against the Pacific Fleet at Pearl. Launched from aircraft carriers, hundreds of planes pounded the naval base and left it a fiery ruin. They damaged or sunk sixteen ships, including all eight battleships. They bombed some 200 planes on the runway at nearby airfields. More than 2,000 died.

The President called it a "date that will live in infamy."

Being on the *Kennedy* at the time, Charlie had missed it.

Three days after the attack on Pearl, the Japanese bombed the naval base at Cavite, where the Asiatic Fleet was stationed, and flattened it.

Cavite's destruction must have been a real horror, but Charlie envied Rusty for having lived through it. He'd missed that too. He'd missed the Battle of the Coral Sea and the victory in June at Midway, where the Navy sank four Japanese aircraft carriers and a heavy cruiser. He'd missed the invasion of Guadalcanal in August and the devastating response.

Now he was finally getting into the war, just in time for the big win.

"We're on offense now," he said, sounding tough. "We'll have them beat in no time."

Rusty shook his head. "Don't talk like that in front of the guys."

"Huh?" Had he said something wrong? "Why not?"

"I got news for you, Charlie. We're in for a long war." When Charlie huffed at that, he explained, "Everybody back home looks at the Japs as a nation of slant-eyed heathens with buckteeth and bad eyesight, but they're damned good at war."

"You don't hate them?"

Rusty glared. "They killed friends of mine, Charlie. Of course, I hate them. I hate their rotten guts. The point is they've got good skippers, and they're tough as nails. They'll do anything for their emperor. A good thing to know if you're going to fight them."

"Roger that," Charlie muttered.

"Their equipment's also better than ours. We're playing catch up. In the meantime, we're fighting in a leaky sewer pipe with faulty torpedoes. We fight to keep the boat going more than we fight the Japs. She's older than most of her crew."

He sagged in his seat, a tired old man in his early twenties, and again Charlie envied his experience and even his weariness. What had he seen? So much had happened. He was there.

"I hear you," Charlie told him. "But you make it sound like we're going to lose."

"We've got good men. As good as theirs, if not better. We've got that going for us."

"God bless you men," Kate said from the driver's seat. "We're grateful you're here."

After Pearl, the Japanese Empire had captured the Philippines, Guam, Wake Island, Hong Kong, French Indochina, Burma, and most of the Dutch East Indies. They began building up for an invasion of Australia. They were slowly isolating Australia and threatening the supply lanes from America. They'd already bombed Darwin and shelled Sydney.

The Australians were terrified.

"Amen, Mrs. Moore," Rusty perked up, his ill humor gone. "At least we have God on our side, though he works in mysterious ways." Then he turned to Charlie and said, "Do yourself a favor and don't do that gung-ho thing in front of the captain."

"Wilco." Charlie decided to take his advice. He wouldn't give up his enthusiasm, but he'd keep it to himself. If the captain could be a cool customer, so could he.

CHAPTER THREE
THE CAPTAIN

The party was in full swing. Red-faced officers and pretty Aussie girls laughed while a record played a hopping tune that Charlie recognized as "Dupree Shake Dance" by Champion Jack Dupree. Cigarette smoke hung in the air. The scene struck him as a bit unreal. On his long journey across the Pacific, he'd prepared to be thrown headfirst into hardship and combat, not drinking and flirting with leggy blondes.

It reminded him the war was a big place with plenty of downtime and even some good times. He stowed his service cap and bag in a coat closet, ready to do as the Romans.

Rusty introduced him to the boat's new executive officer, a tall and brooding man named Reynolds, and the officers of the S-37, another submarine receiving repairs.

Charlie barely registered their faces, his eyes on the captain.

Lieutenant-Commander J.R. Kane stood by the window in service khakis, drink in his hand, cornered by three Aussie girls wearing colorful sleeveless dresses and holding tall glasses of amber-colored beer. He smiled as he told some story. They looked at him in awe.

Rusty nudged Charlie with a smile and said, "Come on. I'll introduce you to the Old Man."

"Old Man" was a nickname for ship captains. The truth was Kane was only a few years older than Charlie. Not even thirty, and he already had his own command. If for nothing else, Charlie respected him for that.

War was hell, but it was a time of opportunity for naval officers, especially the Pacific War, which so far had mainly been a naval conflict. New ships required crews staffed by officers adaptable to new technology and warfare doctrines.

Kane was clean shaven and good looking in a rugged way—John Wayne playing a submarine skipper. He wore dolphins on his clean starched shirt, signifying he was qualified in submarine warfare. His hands didn't shake, but every so often his eyes clenched in a pronounced blink. A nervous tic?

"Pardon the interruption, ladies," Rusty cut in. "Captain, I'd like you to meet Charles Harrison, a young man destined for great things. I ran into him at the boat and recruited him on the spot with vague promises of glory."

"Glad to have you aboard, Harrison," the captain said.

"Thank you, sir," Charlie said.

As they were indoors and he didn't have his peaked cap on, Charlie didn't offer a salute. They shook hands while the women appraised him and giggled.

"I trust you're rested and ready for duty," Kane said.

"Very much so, sir."

"We lost two of our officers. Drafted to new

10

construction."

The pigboats were being retired. They were built in an era when submarines were thought of as coastal defense vessels. Doctrine had changed with new technology. The new fleet boats functioned as their name implied—to operate as part of a fleet. They were bigger, had a longer range at sea, and fired newer torpedoes. They also had brand new machinery, the latest instrumentation and, last but not least, air conditioning.

The captain added, "I hope you know what you're in for, signing up with a pigboat."

"I went where I was needed, sir. I wanted to get in the fight as soon as possible."

"You'll change your mind after a few weeks of heat and stink and no air conditioning."

"If she fires torpedoes, I'll be happy to be aboard."

"She does," Rusty cut in. "They just don't always shoot straight."

"You served on a destroyer," the captain noted.

"That's right," Charlie said. "The *Kennedy*, stationed in the Atlantic."

"Then the Japs bomb Pearl, and you up for a transfer to a pigboat in the Pacific. Just wondering what you were thinking, making such a big change."

"The Japs attacked us, sir. I wanted to pay them back. Take the fight straight to 'em."

"I figured as much. But why a submarine?"

"The Japs made a big mistake at Pearl," Charlie explained. "They didn't bomb the submarine piers. They didn't hit the

11

fuel dumps, torpedo plant, or machine shops. The boats at Pearl and Cavite were still in the game, and I knew they'd be on offense."

"Interesting line of thought. Very logical." Kane gave Charlie an appraising look then added, "So where are you from, Harrison?"

"Tiburon. A coastal town north of San Francisco. Across the bay."

"San Fran, eh? You must have spent some time on boats."

"I grew up on boats, sir. Fishing and crabbing."

"We'll have to compare notes. I'm a bit of a fisherman myself."

"I'd like that, sir," Charlie said warmly, but he chafed at the small talk. "Any word on the mission, sir? Are we going to Guadalcanal?"

In August, the Marines landed on Guadalcanal and two other islands. They captured the Japanese airfield and renamed it Henderson Field. This served two strategic aims. First, to prevent the Japanese from using the islands to threaten supply and communication lines between America and Australia. Second, to provide bases from which the Allies could neutralize or capture Rabaul.

The Americans and Japanese had been fighting over it by land, sea, and air ever since. A fight to the death in which neither side showed mercy. Guadalcanal had become a meat grinder.

The captain smiled. "Enough talk about work. Let's blow off some steam. I see you haven't gotten a drink yet. Rusty will help you rectify that."

Charlie was being dismissed. He let Rusty drag him to the other side of the room.

"I'm a stupid idiot," Charlie said. It had been dumb to ask the captain about the mission in front of civilians. He'd played it cool but then revealed himself as an overeager beaver.

Rusty smiled as he poured them both a glass of Emu Bitter beer. "It's called the 'Silent Service' for a reason, brother."

"I guess I'm still learning."

"Drink up." Rusty raised his glass and said gravely, "To all ships in the Navy. To all ladies of our land. May the former be well rigged and the latter be well manned."

CHAPTER FOUR

RIG FOR SEA

Under a hot sun, the S-55 buzzed with activity. Dusty men in blue shirts and dirty dungarees swarmed across her deck. Trucks pumped fresh water and fuel through thick hoses into the submarine's tanks. The air reeked with thick diesel stench. She lay low in the water, with a draft of sixteen feet between the waterline and the keel. Surfaced as she was, she displaced 900 tons of water. Sailors passed boxes of frozen meat, coffee, and canned fruit and vegetables down the hatch, where they were stowed in every nook and cranny. The quartermaster raced about with a clipboard and marked it all down in his ledger.

Shore patrol pulled up and dumped two half-conscious men on the dock. The sailors jeered at their comrades and called them skates—loafers. One stood, grinned, and waved—and then promptly fell over, still drunk from his last night of shore leave. Charlie shook his head and got back to work. The chief of the boat, a big, burly man named Dobbs, would see to those men.

Charlie's responsibilities included gunnery officer. If the S-55 ever needed to surface to sink a merchant or, God forbid, trade punches with a destroyer, it was his job to make sure the gun and its crew were ready to fire and do so with effect. As for himself, he'd be on the bridge during the action, spotting for the gun crew while exposed to enemy fire— though, in a gun action, nowhere was safe.

For now, it was his duty to double-check the equipment. He made sure the barrel was plugged tight and the hinged cover over the breech properly secured. The plug and cover ensured the firing mechanisms didn't get wet after submerging, which would render the gun useless when their lives depended on it.

Nearby, a group of sailors guided a new torpedo, hanging from a crane, down the weapons hatch. The men glanced at Charlie and turned away. "Skimmer puke," he heard. A derogatory term submariners used for guys in surface ships. He frowned at the insult.

On the whole, submariners were shaping up as a clannish breed. They alone fought under the surface; anything on it was a potential enemy.

A sailor approached Charlie. "Mr. Harrison?"

"Yeah?"

"I was told to get the keys to the boat from you."

"The keys?"

"Yes, sir. Captain can't put to sea without 'em."

Charlie noticed the men continuing their duties while suppressing laughter. He returned his gaze to the sailor, whom he now knew was a greenhorn, and asked his name.

"Billy. Billy Ford," said the blond-haired kid.

With as much gravity as he could muster, Charlie said,

"Thank you, Billy. The captain entrusted the keys to me. I'll pass them on to him. Carry on."

"Aye, aye, sir." The recruit ran off on some other fool's errand.

Rusty appeared at Charlie's side and grinned. "The snipe hunt never gets old. You know, you might have kept it going for a laugh. Sent him on to me, maybe."

"On another day, I might have. Today—I'm new here too, Rusty. I guess I sympathized."

"Anybody looking for sympathy in this navy can find it in the dictionary between shit and syphilis. Next time, think about playing along. It would go a long way with the crew."

Charlie said, "They'll either warm up to me, or they won't."

"They're a tight-knit bunch. You might think about how you're going to earn their respect."

"In the Navy I come from, the rank is respected."

"It is," Rusty said. "But on a submarine, it helps if the man is too. The thing is, every one of these guys, from the captain down to the idiot electrician mates, is vital to our survival. Every man on the boat is a specialist. And one of them is going to keep his head during the next heavy attack and stop a leak or do something else that'll save us all."

He added, "Take that joker over there, for example." He pointed to the large, tattooed sailor who'd called Charlie a skimmer puke. "Machinist's Mate John Braddock. We took a hell of a pounding by a destroyer on the retreat from the Philippines and came close to losing the boat. He stood in hellish heat and smoke in the motor room for hours and kept

17

an overheating bearing lubed with an oil gun until we completed repairs. Simple as that, he saved us."

If the boat had lost the starboard motor, she wouldn't have been able to control depth and maintain speed. It's very possible she would have gone to the bottom. On the S-55, heroes didn't charge singlehanded against enemy machine gun nests. They turned wrenches.

Charlie nodded, appreciating the perspective. "Good man."

"If you say so. The guy may be a hero, but he's also a grade-A asshole."

"I get it, Rusty. Tell me one thing. I keep hearing the guys talking about some difficult crewman called Frankie. A real heavyweight. Who is he?"

Rusty laughed. "A heavyweight, yeah. Frankie can be a real bitch."

"You mean Frankie's a woman? Who is she?"

"Frankie's the boat, Charlie. See all the work done on her? Bride of Frankenstein."

Reynolds approached. "Hey, you guys!" He appeared to be bursting with good news. "Did you hear the Japs surrendered?"

Charlie started. "What? No!"

The exec's smile disappeared. "Then get back to work, you jerks. There's a war on."

Rusty turned to Charlie and shrugged. "Duty calls. 'Ours is not to reason why.'"

Charlie got back to it. He smiled to himself. Hazing and berating. Welcome to the Navy. Aside from maybe Rusty,

18

nobody here was going to be his friend. The realization freed him. He didn't have to make anybody like him.

But Rusty was right about one thing. It was important they respect him.

First the rank, then the man. And not by playing along with their jokes. Instead, he'd do his duty to the letter, and they'd never see him flinch.

CHAPTER FIVE
ANGLES AND DANGLES

At 1300, the last crew members boarded the submarine, which went through a battery of final equipment checks. Charlie climbed the metal sail that housed the conning tower and joined the captain on the bridge. All compartments reported they were manned. The S-55 was ready to get underway.

The captain acknowledged each report with an offhand, "Very well." Then he ordered the control room to make way, "Back one-third."

"Back one-third, aye," came the reply through the intercom.

The S-55's big diesel engines pulled the boat away from the pier and tender with a puff of smoke. Her whistle pierced the air. The repair ship's sailors leaned on the rails and called out, "Give 'em hell, boys! Good hunting!"

The captain snorted at that. "Knowing this old boat, we'll be back in an hour."

Charlie suppressed a grin. This was it. His war had officially begun.

The New Farm Wharf fell away. Frankie blew her whistle

again and entered the current of the Brisbane River. Aussies walking to work in the city waved as the submarine returned to the war. An old cobber cupped his hands around his mouth and shouted, "Good-o! Sink one for me, Yanks!"

The captain asked, "What's the most effective tactic the U-boats use, Harrison?"

"Wolf packs, sir. One boat draws off the escorts while the rest move in to sink the merchants. The Nazi skippers are good at coordinating their attacks."

"We could use that," Kane said. "First, we need to build more boats, don't we?"

He was right. There were only about a hundred submarines in the whole Navy, and many of them were old and slow like the S-55.

"Time to buy more war bonds, sir," Charlie said.

The captain smirked at that.

Water foaming at her bow, the submarine entered Moreton Bay. Charlie scanned the brilliant blue waters and pristine beaches. He whistled at the view.

"All right," said the captain. "Let's give the old girl a good shakedown and see if she leaks." He raised his voice. "Clear the topsides."

Charlie followed the men down the ladder into the conning tower and then into the control room. The quartermaster closed the hatch behind them and spun the wheel to secure it.

"Hatch secured!" the quartermaster called down.

The crowded control room reeked of diesel. Charlie scanned the men:

The planesmen with their hands on brass wheels for controlling the planes, plates that angled to control the bow and stern and either tilt the boat or keep her level—

The manifoldmen at the valves that pushed high-pressure air into the ballast tanks to provide buoyancy and make the boat rise, or flooded them with seawater to make the boat heavy for a dive—

The helmsman with his hands on the wheel that steered the boat—

The telephone talker who relayed messages across the boat by sound-powered phone—

The soundman peering around the corner from the radio shack in the corner of the control room, where he listened for enemy contacts—

The chief of the boat, the senior enlisted man aboard, his thick arms folded across his barrel chest, watching over his sailors—

The officers who watched the captain—

And the Old Man who watched over them all.

Whatever fears Charlie felt about combat disappeared. He felt safe with this captain and these men, each competent and experienced in his specialty.

"Rig for dive," Kane said.

The diving alarm klaxon blasted three times. The main induction valve, which fed air into the boat for the crew and the engines, clanged shut. The diesel engines cut out. The electric motors were engaged by the batteries, which powered the boat while it was submerged.

All departments reported being ready to dive.

23

"Air in the banks, shit in the tanks," Reynolds told the captain.

"Very well. Dive. Three degrees down bubble. Forty-five feet."

The manifoldmen opened the vents to flood the ballast tanks with seawater and make the boat heavy. The planesmen turned their wheels in opposite directions to angle the boat down. Charlie enjoyed watching them work. From a purely technical standpoint, a submarine, even an old boat like this, was a marvel. A vessel able to move in three dimensions through water.

At Submarine School, he'd had the opportunity to work the planes on an even older, even smaller R-class sub. Being in control of a sub was fun. A toy for grownups playing at war; except out here, they weren't playing.

In sixty seconds flat, the S-55 disappeared into Moreton Bay. They were underwater.

The submarine dived to periscope depth.

"Report leaks," the captain said.

"Motor room reports a minor leak," the telephone talker reported.

"I'll take a look," Rusty said and left the room.

"Very well." Kane added, "How's our final trim?"

"We've got good trim," Reynolds answered. The boat held neutral buoyancy with an even keel, well balanced in the water.

Charlie heard hammering somewhere in the sub. That was Rusty, checking the integrity of plates that had been welded over hull pitting.

The engineering officer returned to the control room and nodded to the captain.

"So far, so good," Kane said. He rubbed his chin and smiled at Rusty. "Moment of truth."

"Neptune, hear our prayer," Rusty said.

"Take her down. One hundred fifty feet."

The crew glanced at each other. Charlie realized they were apprehensive. It confused him. The first generation of S-class submarines were tested to a depth of more than 200 feet. What was the problem?

It didn't take him long to come up with the answer. Frankie was old. She just couldn't go that deep anymore without major flooding.

Reynolds read the depth gauge. "Passing eighty feet."

Planes rigged, the boat tilted as she glided into the depths.

"Passing 100 feet," the XO said.

The deeper she went, the more pressure the water outside exerted on the hull.

A major leak, and they'd have to return to the tender for more refitting. Charlie fidgeted. They were only a few miles from Moreton Island and, around it, a path to the open sea!

"Passing 130 feet."

The old boat's hull creaked, sounding like she might burst at the seams. The men tensed. Charlie sensed the change in atmosphere and tensed as well.

The boat leveled off.

"Final trim, 150 feet," Reynolds said.

Kane raised his eyebrows at Rusty.

Rusty grinned ear to ear. "We're dry, Captain."

Charlie sighed quietly. The S-55 was ready to head out to her patrol station.

"Looks like we're in business," Kane said. "This old sea wolf is itching for a fight."

Around the control room, the men smiled.

He gave orders to return to the surface.

On the surface, the soundman radioed back to the tender at New Farm Wharf that the S-55 was ready. Less than an hour later, the boat was released for patrol.

Kane set a course for the open sea. Then he keyed the 1MC box and said, "Attention. This is the captain."

His voice reverberated throughout the boat on the public-address loudspeakers.

"As you know, the Jap Navy has set up a defensive wall around their empire. When we took Guadalcanal, we stuck our foot in their door. The Japs are doing everything they can to slam it shut. The Marines are hanging on by a thread. Now it's time for Frankie to do her part."

He cleared his throat and went on, "Our patrol orders are to proceed to Guadalcanal, alert the fleet of enemy movements, and sink Jap ships. Everything the Japs throw at our boys on Guadalcanal—every soldier, every bomb, every gallon of gas—must go by sea. It's our job to make sure they never make it to their destination. It's our duty to send every Jap ship we find, and every Jap on it, to the bottom."

CHAPTER SIX

THE SLOT

The captain ordered the sailors of section one to man their stations. The submarine crew was divided into three sections. Each was able to run all of the boat's systems for a four-hour watch; if it came to a fight, the most experienced hands reported to duty. Charlie was assigned to section two.

The S-55 carefully threaded the minefields guarding the entrance to Moreton Bay while lookouts kept a sharp eye for enemy submarines that hoped to catch somebody napping. Then the boat reached the Coral Sea and submerged into the deep. The helmsman set a course for 005º True. North by east to the Solomon Islands.

Two 600-HP diesel engines propelled the boat while she was surfaced. On a calm sea, Frankie cruised at a maximum speed of 14.5 knots, or over sixteen land miles per hour. With a full bunkerage of 170 tons of fuel, she could range up to 5,000 miles.

But only at night. During daylight hours, Japanese seaplanes easily spotted submarines on the surface and, in the brightly lit Pacific, even at periscope depth. Lacking air-detection radar, the S-55 patrolled deep on battery power during daylight hours. During this time, two big electric motors, powered by a 120-cell battery, drove the boat at a speed of a sluggish 2.5 knots.

With limited speed, fuel, and provisions, Frankie had endurance for a thirty-day patrol.

Kane called a meeting of his officers in the wardroom. The men sat around the small square table, surrounded by dull wood-paneled walls, while Nimuel, the Filipino steward, served coffee. Reynolds pulled a wilted pack of Lucky Strikes from his breast pocket and lit one with a match.

The captain laid out a chart on the table. "The Slot."

Charlie studied the map of the Solomon Islands, which ran a thousand miles from New Britain and New Ireland in the northwest down to Guadalcanal and San Cristobal in the southeast. The main Japanese air and naval base was at Rabaul on New Britain. Between Rabaul and Guadalcanal lay a scattering of islands, through which a line of water formed a natural roadway—the Slot.

"As you know, the Japs run reinforcements down the Slot to Guadalcanal," Kane went on. "Not to mention give the Marines and Henderson Airfield a real pounding about anytime they feel like it. The Japs are using their fastest destroyers. They can run down to Guadalcanal at night, when our planes can't see them, and be back in Rabaul in time for sushi."

"The Tokyo Express," Rusty said.

"Right. So many ships on both sides have been sunk, the skimmers are calling Savo Sound 'Iron Bottom.'" He shot a glance at Charlie. "No offense, Harrison."

"None taken, sir," Charlie said, suppressing a frown. The "skimmers" remark didn't sting; the apology did. It reminded him his boatmates didn't yet consider him a real submariner.

"Admiral Lockwood is deploying submarines as pickets around the island. We're going to report enemy movements down the Slot and see if we can bag a few tin cans of our own."

"What's our patrol station?" Rusty asked.

Kane tapped the map with his finger. "Here. Savo Island. Less than ten miles off the western tip of Guadalcanal. Right in the thick of things. We'll have tin cans flying at us every night."

Reynolds looked like he wanted to spit. "I thought we'd be killing Japs on this patrol."

The captain eyed him. "That's the goddamn idea, Reynolds."

"We should be ranging up the channel." Reynolds blew a stream of smoke and stabbed his cigarette into the ashtray. "Go to Rabaul if we have to. Get at their merchants and transports. Take the fight straight to the yellow sons of bitches."

Charlie agreed with the exec. Frankie was an old girl but still dangerous. She had the element of surprise on her side. But in a picket line, with the enemy becoming aware of her presence, that advantage would quickly evaporate.

The best use of submarines was to attack the enemy's shipping. Japan's rapidly growing empire depended on sea transport. Food, metal ores, rubber, and oil to her home islands. Reinforcements and war materiel flowing back out to her conquests. Sinking her merchant fleet would strangle her economy, not to mention tie up destroyers for escort duty, and bring a speedy end to the war.

"We have our orders," Kane said.

"Picket duty with this old boat," Reynolds snarled. "Taking on destroyers and cruisers. Like bringing a knife to a gunfight."

The exec's face had gone dark with black hatred. He wasn't just upset about the strategy. Charlie suspected a personal motive. A vendetta against the Japanese.

"We have our orders," the captain repeated with quiet menace. He stared at the man, daring him to continue. When Reynolds said nothing, he added, "Now let's go sink some Jap ships. We'll surface at dark. Dinner will be at midnight and breakfast just after dawn. The usual schedule."

Nimuel had returned with his coffee pot. "We're having minced beef in tomato sauce," he announced, oblivious to the tension in the room. He refreshed their coffee mugs.

Charlie nodded as he drank his coffee.

The captain added, "Harrison, you'll be OOD on surfacing and officer of the first watch."

Specifically, the second dog watch, from 1800 to 2000.

Charlie blinked. Watch duty entailed entering the bridge via the conning tower hatch and scanning the darkness for enemy ships. Standard routine.

As officer of the deck, however, he'd have both authority and responsibility for the safety of the boat and its crew. If he ordered the boat to dive or change course, she would on his say-so.

He swallowed hard and said, "Aye, aye, sir."

CHAPTER SEVEN
WHY WE FIGHT

The S-55 was a small world, a loud and smelly machine inhabited by industrious rats. She was no boat, but the sailors called her one because the first submarines were no bigger than boats. Habits die hard in the Navy. Still, she was a small world.

From bow to stern, the six major compartments included the torpedo, battery, control, engine, motor, and maneuvering rooms. The crew slept among boxes of food above the battery room next to the wardroom, and the officers in two state rooms aft.

Charlie studied the crew's rhythm and did his best to join the flow, but more often than not, he caused pileups in the passageways. The sailors only worsened his rising embarrassment by courteously mumbling, "Excuse me, sir. Careful there, sir." Then Braddock barked, "Make a hole, sir! Working Navy!" which made him feel strangely happy and try even harder.

The R-class submarine he'd maneuvered at Submarine School had been even smaller, but he'd only served on it for a few hours at a time. It had been like driving a car. He didn't *live* in it. This felt perpetual. Unless he washed out, which was possible, he'd serve on a boat like this until the end of the war. Which, if Rusty was any authority on the subject, promised to be a long one.

By 1600, any trepidation he'd felt about being officer of the deck on the first watch fled with his growing longing to be topside again. On the U.S.S. *Kennedy*, he'd seen greenhorns puke over the gunwales as they fought to get their sea legs. Charlie had never suffered seasickness. Now, on a submarine, he felt mounting claustrophobia and cursed himself for it.

He was sweating buckets. His heart galloped.

"You got yourself into this mess," he mumbled to himself.

He'd begin his watch at 1800, about twenty minutes before sunset. Until then, he decided to lie down in his bunk and rest. He needed to relax before he started clawing at the nearest bulkhead.

Charlie found Rusty lying on his bunk reading a book. He threw himself into his own bunk, closed his eyes against the nausea, and focused on his breathing.

"War is hell," Rusty said.

Charlie took a deep breath and said, "What are you reading?"

"An Edgar Allen Poe story about a man who's buried alive." Then he laughed. "Just kidding. A lot of guys start banging on the hatch after a few hours on the boat. You'll get used to it." He didn't need to add, "Or you won't." Either way, Charlie's suffering was temporary. "I'm reading Gibbon's *Decline and Fall of the Roman Empire*. The good news

34

is, if the Japanese conquer the world, they'll grow soft after a few thousand years and collapse."

"Sounds like a good one," Charlie said, sweating. "I'm surprised we're cruising submerged today. The Jap planes don't range this far south, right?"

"The captain wants to get the crew used to the routine well before we reach our patrol station. We only give up a day and half of patrolling in exchange."

"The captain's a cautious man."

"Prudent," Rusty clarified. "He certainly is. He works this boat like he plays chess, very analytical. What do you think of our man, Reynolds? Talk about fire in the belly."

Charlie opened his eyes and raised himself onto one elbow. "I like him."

"His last command sank in the Banda Sea on the way down from the Philippines. The 56. A Jap destroyer held the boat under until she had to surface. Then the Japs sank her. Reynolds was the only man left to tell the tale. The 44 picked him up. He should have gone home, but somehow, he conned the Navy into putting him on another submarine."

"Shit, I didn't know all that," Charlie said. What a tale! He was even more curious about the man now. "Anyway, he seems smart. I think he has some good ideas on how to win the war."

"He's the aggressive sort, I'll give you that."

"He's right. We should go to Rabaul and sink ships."

Japan's survival depended on the steady flow of raw materials, armies, and war materiel traveling by sea. The day after the surprise attack at Pearl, Admiral Hart declared unrestricted submarine warfare against Japan, a major change in naval doctrine.

Germany had been widely condemned during the Great War for doing just that. The London Naval Treaty allowed submarines to sink merchants, but they had to abide by prize rules. That is, the boat had to surface and put the crew somewhere safe before sinking it.

A submarine could barely fit its own crew and couldn't take many prisoners. Merchants had destroyer escorts that could quickly sink a submarine trying to abide by the rules. As a result, all of the major powers were now disregarding the treaty.

Sinking Japan's merchants wasn't pleasant work, but it could save countless American lives. At this moment, America and Japan were locked in a merciless fight to the death. Total war.

"Go to Rabaul and sink ships," Rusty echoed. "Just like that, huh?"

"Isn't that how it's supposed to work?"

"Assuming Frankie makes it there, our broke-dick fire control computer doesn't automatically set the gyros on the torpedoes. We have to set the gyros by hand. But they're old, so the spindles stick. They taught you fire control in New London, right? The whole nine yards?"

"Of course."

Fire control entailed fast calculation of angles and distances in combat. In a basic problem, you had two objects—you and your target—at X distance apart and moving at different speeds (Y and Z) and directions (A and

B). Given X, Y, Z, A, and B, all of which might suddenly change, how do you get a torpedo across distance X to hit the target?

It wasn't nearly as easy as it might seem, so fleet submarines were equipped with torpedo data computers, which automatically fed firing solutions to the torpedo gyros, which in turn controlled the angle of torpedo travel.

Rusty said, "Here's how we do it out here in the real world on a broken-down S-boat. We set up a zero gyro angle shot; we have to shoot our fish straight ahead. We estimate the target's speed, add three to come up with a lead angle, and shoot at that point from between a thousand and 1,500 yards. Sometimes with visual contact, but often going only by sound bearings."

In other words, it was all rule of thumb on the S-55. Half-blind bow and arrow shooting.

Rusty added, "And all that with a target that is zigzagging and flanked by destroyers pinging like crazy with their sonar and dropping random depth charges. With a boat that can only go two and a half knots while underwater, ten if we're willing to drain the battery fast."

"Right," Charlie said, taking it all in.

"If we get a shot, we then hope the old torpedo doesn't go erratic and fly away, or worse, circle back and sink us. No wonder the Navy takes captains off their boats after five patrols. The pressure is incredible. The captain's smart to play it safe. He knows what he's doing."

Charlie sagged. "What are we doing here then?"

"Holding the line until more fleet boats show up. Sink a

ship if we can with what we have. Tie up as many enemy ships on escort duty that we're able to. Otherwise, do what we're told and try not to get killed." Rusty perked up, inspired. "Want to see why I'm here?" He dug into his breast pocket and handed Charlie a photo.

Rusty's wife was a looker. She'd carefully dressed, styled her hair, and put on makeup for the shot. She stood on a beach, the wind threatening to sweep the hat off her head. She held a baby in one arm and blew a kiss at the camera lens.

Rusty said, "That's my wife, Lucy. And that's my son, Russell Junior. He's two now. Already a smartass, just like his old man."

"She's a doll, Rusty. On the level. Get kid too." He handed the photo back.

Rusty smiled at it a few moments before putting it away. "You got a girl, Charlie?"

"Yeah. I mean, no, not anymore."

"Sorry to hear it. What happened with you two?"

"Nothing," Charlie said. "I mean, Evelyn and I were good together. We were going to get married. Then Pearl got bombed, and the war started. I broke things off before I went to Submarine School."

"You did? *Why*, man?"

"I thought she'd distract me. I wanted to focus entirely on the war. On my duty."

Feeling self-conscious, he didn't add the bigger reason. He'd come here to find himself. Specifically, what Charles F. Harrison was made of and how far he could go in the Navy.

To survive—no, to win—he knew he'd have to face mortal danger. He didn't believe he could make the right decisions in the face of death while Evie waited for him back home.

"You're a real go-getter, aren't you," Rusty said. "Tough, smart, and ambitious. I know that about you already. You could go far in the Navy."

Charlie flushed at the compliment. "Jeez, Rusty."

"But you're wrapped a little tight, and it shows. You have to loosen up to make it in the submarines. Take things as they come. A man who fights for an idea is dangerous. A man like Reynolds. He'd send us all to the bottom just to sink a stinking Jap ship."

"I want to be at my best. We're fighting a war."

"I hear that, but I'm telling you as a friend, you made a mistake ending things with that girl. A man's got to have something real to fight for. Something for which you need to live as well as for which you're willing to die." He patted his breast pocket. "Me, I'm fighting for them. And I'll survive for them. I want to win the war, and I want to get home."

Charlie didn't know what to say to that. Rusty turned over and fell fast asleep.

He lay with his head on his hands and stared up at the harsh metal bulkhead for a while, thinking of Evie and what he was doing here. Was Rusty right? He'd had such clarity of purpose when he told her he needed to end things so he could focus on winning the war. He'd worked so hard to get here that he hadn't had much time or energy to think about anything else. Now that he was here, in the thick of it, he felt lonely. He began to miss her. Rusty's speech had stirred him up.

He daydreamed about a sunny picnic with her on the hill overlooking the Bay. They'd found an ancient native rock carving and guessed at its meaning. The guessing became a game of wild speculation that had them laughing. *Men's Room,* she guessed. *Women's Lingerie. Kilroy Was Here.* She had a sharp wit; she could always make him laugh and, at the same time, believe in himself. Believe he could do or be anything as long as she was watching him.

The submarine's walls stopped closing in. A deep, dreamless sleep overcame him. After what seemed like seconds, a hand shook him awake. He'd fallen asleep on that sunny hillside, and Evie was waking him up so they could go home. He looked around with alarm, unsure where he was. Then he remembered.

He was back on the S-55, and it was time for the watch.

CHAPTER EIGHT

DOG WATCH

After Charlie finished his coffee, he reported to the control room, which had been rigged for red. All normal lamps had been extinguished. Dim red lamps, turned on to help the men's eyes adapt for night vision, cast the room in a menacing glow.

"Lookouts to the control room," Charlie instructed the chief petty officer.

The captain wore a sou'wester hat and was putting on oilskins. "Planes, forty-five feet. Time for a look-see."

"Forty-five feet, aye, Captain," came the response.

At that depth, he ordered, "Up scope."

He crouched, pulled the handles down, and pressed his eyes against the rubber eyepiece, straightening his legs as the periscope rose. Water rained on him from the periscope's upper bearings. He clapped the handles back into place.

"Fogged again," he said sourly. The captain couldn't see anything through the fogged-up scope. "Down scope. All compartments, rig to surface."

The telephone talker said into the phone, "Maneuvering room, on surfacing, answer bells on two main engines. Put one main on charge."

Once the boat returned to the surface, the batteries would disengage the electric motors. One of the diesel engines would power the motors. The other would dump amps into the battery. After the battery recharged, the second engine would be put on propulsion, as well. Compressors would replenish the air used to blow the ballast tanks and achieve buoyancy.

Meanwhile, Charlie's three lookouts had gathered. They wore binoculars around their necks and otherwise seemed ready for their important job. One of them was the greenhorn, Billy Ford.

"I was told to keep an eye out for the mail buoy, Mr. Harrison," the kid said in a quiet voice.

"Mail buoy?"

"Yeah," Billy said with surprise that an officer didn't know about it. "The Navy put our mail on a buoy in these waters. I'll find it for you. Jeez, I can't wait to get mail!"

Another snipe hunt. Braddock's work, probably. Did the man know there was a war on? Charlie said, "The mail drop was canceled, Billy. Keep your eyes peeled for the enemy."

Billy appeared crestfallen. "Aye, aye, Mr. Harrison."

"Forward engine room, secure ventilation," the captain said. "All compartments, shut the bulkhead flappers."

The telephone talker reported, "Ready to surface in every respect, Captain."

"Very well," Kane grumbled. "Surface."

The surfacing alarm sounded throughout the boat. The manifoldmen blew the main ballast tanks. High-pressure air buoyed the boat. Charlie ascended to the conning tower, followed by the quartermaster and lookouts.

The two glass portholes revealed inky black nothing. The water foamed as the S-55 broke the surface. Charlie fingered the strap of the binoculars around his neck. By this point, he was more afraid of letting down his boatmates than he was of the Japanese.

"Open the hatch," Kane said. "Open the main induction."

With a rubber mallet, the quartermaster removed the dogs locking the hatch. He spun the wheel and cracked it open. Air pressure had built up inside the boat while it was submerged. It rushed past Charlie with a howl, forcing him to pause. Then he climbed onto the bridge.

After spending part of the day underwater in hot diesel stink, the clean, relatively cool air and fresh smell of the sea revived him. He raised his binoculars and scanned the dark in all directions. The moon hadn't risen yet; the darkness was complete.

He didn't see any enemy ships. Frankly, he didn't see much of anything.

"All clear!" he shouted down the hatch. "Lookouts to the bridge."

The men climbed out and took their stations.

Then they watched.

It was tedious, and then boring, and then more tedious. But necessary. The sea was a big place, but it had become crowded with warships. If an enemy destroyer caught them by surprise in the dark, they'd be a sitting duck. The same probably went for friendly warships. If an Allied ship found the S-55, the captain might shoot first and wonder whom he sank later.

If the submariners wanted to stay alive, they had to stay vigilant.

Soon, the men got to chatting. Fredericks started ribbing Peters about passing up a date with a pretty Aussie girl who'd done everything to get his attention short of asking him out directly.

"I didn't like her," Peters protested. "I liked her sister, Beth."

"Buddy, you must be the only sailor in the whole goddamn Navy who's picky about women," Fredericks laughed. "You had a bird in the hand, so to speak."

"Worth two in the bush!" Billy Ford crowed.

Fredericks said, "See? Even the new kid knows which end is up in this Navy."

"You don't get it," Peters told them. "I'm going to marry Beth when this is all over."

"Does she know she's engaged to you, hotshot?"

"Silence," Charlie said.

The men clammed up.

He added, "Keep your eyes peeled."

An hour rolled by while Frankie continued to make way across the Coral Sea. Charlie's mind wandered. Billy's talk about a mail buoy made him wonder if he should write Evie a letter. He decided that this was an important thing for him to do. He just didn't know what to say. Did he want her back? Did he deserve her trust?

If only he could talk to her again, he'd know exactly what

to do.

"Sound contact," a voice said over the intercom. It was Reynolds. "Three thousand yards off the starboard bow, bearing oh-eight-five True." True was in reference to true north, as opposed to a relative bearing based on the direction of Frankie's bow.

That was Charlie's sector. He squinted into the dark, looking for a telltale smudge that might be an enemy ship.

"Starboard clear," he reported back. "No visual contact."

"Soundman now says it's a submarine," Reynolds told him.

Charlie checked the water for the wake of an incoming torpedo. Microorganisms in the seawater, called dinoflagellates, produced a short burst of light when agitated. For them, it was a self-defense mechanism. It also served to alert surface vessels of incoming torpedoes.

The water remained dark.

The next order came quickly: "Clear the bridge!"

Charlie continued to look while the men went down the hatch. Then he turned.

The hatch slammed shut at his feet.

The boat was already going down, sliding gracefully into the black water.

"Control room," he said. "Reynolds! Personnel still on the bridge!"

Inside the sub, he knew, the diving alarm was blaring, and the men in the control room were all talking. Did they hear him?

If this was another practical joke, it was going too far.

Whoever among his lookouts did it, Charlie was going to bring him before the mast for punishment.

If he survived this.

He pounded on the hatch until his hand ached. The water washed over the deck. Frankie continued her plunge. The boat disappeared around him as she dived. Sixty seconds. That's all it took for the S-55 to become completely submerged.

"Reynolds!"

This was actually happening. He stood and looked up at the shears. That would be his Alamo. He'd have to climb to gain a precious few seconds. After that, a cold plunge.

The water level rose to the base of the metal sail. The Pacific sprawled at his feet. He felt salt spray in his face. He was about to take a terrifying night swim in the Coral Sea.

No raft, no flare gun, no life jacket.

"Reynolds! Shit. Shit!"

He decided not to climb the shears. He'd gain a few seconds, nothing more.

Wait—the water was going *down*. He was rising.

The S-55 was coming back up.

The hatch opened. The quartermaster shook his head at him and motioned for him to hurry. Trembling, Charlie got down the ladder as fast as he could. The S-55 resumed her dive.

Down in the control room, the soundman said, "Screws fading to the east."

Billy Ford stared at Charlie with wide eyes. "Sorry, Mr. Harrison. I got excited and closed the hatch. I thought you

46

were down." The kid's eyes began to water. "Honest."

Just a greenhorn's dumb mistake. Charlie knew everybody was watching him. Even in his terrified and enraged state, he had enough presence of mind to try to salvage what was left of his dignity. "All right, Billy," he said. "Carry on."

The chief of the boat glared at the kid. "Now get out of here, you stupid idiot. I'll deal with you later." He touched his hat. "It won't happen again, Mr. Harrison. You can take that to the bank."

"Very well, Chief."

Kane smiled at him. Reynolds frowned.

"Eleven seconds, Harrison," the captain said. "That's how long it takes to clear the bridge before we start going down."

"Sorry, sir."

"It's a lesson well learned, I think."

"Certainly, sir."

"By now, you may have some regrets for signing up for service on our little pigboat, but there's no need to commit *hara-kiri*."

The enlisted men grinned at that. Charlie lost his cool and scowled. With the captain's humorous pronouncement, he knew a legend had just been born. The scuttlebutt would take it across the boat and possibly the entire Navy.

Then he smiled at the absurdity of it all. Laughed out loud, much to the captain's amusement.

He now knew exactly what he'd put in his letter to Evie.

CHAPTER NINE
GUN DRILL

After one of his officers nearly took a nighttime swim in the Coral Sea, Captain Kane mercilessly drilled the entire crew to get them into fighting trim. Reynolds was more discriminating; he considered Charlie a potential failure point, another machine to overhaul.

As a result, Charlie was now assistant-everything officer. He practiced every officer duty, even simulated attack approaches. He observed the enlisted men doing their work, from the helmsman who steered the boat to the auxiliarymen who kept her support systems running. He made detailed sketches of the boat's systems in his submarine qualification notebook, from electrical to high-pressure air.

Between the grueling heat, longer hours, and having his ass ridden by the brooding and irritable exec, he was exhausted.

He didn't mind the firehose treatment, though; in fact, he welcomed it. He was learning. Every man on the boat should have been able to perform every other man's duty during an emergency; Charlie realized Submarine School had taught him only a fraction of what there was to know. His claustrophobia faded until he scarcely noticed it. Reynolds and his heavy-handed methods were turning him from a skimmer puke into a dedicated sewer pipe rat.

The executive officer was a hard, moody man with more ghosts in his head than a haunted house. He screamed in his sleep, no doubt reliving the horrifying sinking of the 56. But he was experienced and efficient. Charlie admired him.

Meanwhile, the S-55 continued to cruise north toward the Solomons. By the time she reached her patrol station, Charlie would be ready for combat.

He entered the wardroom at dawn, hoping for a hearty breakfast. The captain and Reynolds were already seated. The captain lit his pipe, filling the room with the rich smell of cherry smoke. Charlie noted again that the exec was the only man on the boat who stayed clean-shaven.

As Charlie took his seat, Reynolds said, "What are you doing, Lieutenant?"

His sleep-addled brain couldn't produce any obvious answer the man would find acceptable. He chose the safe path. "Awaiting orders or instruction, sir."

Reynolds lit a cigarette. "Do you want to kill Japs, Harrison?"

"That's why I'm here, sir."

The captain, much amused, sat back in his chair with his arms crossed.

The exec smiled as well. The smile of a rattlesnake. "How bad do you want to kill Japs, Harrison? So bad you'll do whatever it takes?"

Kane frowned a little at that but said nothing.

Charlie said, "I'll do whatever it takes to help us win this war."

"Good answer, Harrison," the captain said.

"Whatever it takes, huh?" Reynolds said. "Then you'd better quit dogging it and prepare for action."

"Sir?"

The exec looked at his watch. "Wait for it."

Seconds passed while Charlie puzzled over the man's meaning. He glanced at the captain, but Kane's face told him nothing. Then he stiffened as the general alarm honked through the boat.

The quartermaster announced over the public address, "Battle stations, gun action. Deck gun only. All compartments, this is a deck gun drill. Repeat. This is a deck gun drill."

Reynolds blew a long stream of smoke and said, "The 55 is still surfaced." He looked at his watch again. "It's 0623. We'll be diving at 0630. You have until then to fire three shells into the sea. If you're not down the hatch by that time, this time we're leaving you up there—"

Charlie was already out of the room. "Make a hole! Coming through!"

He entered the control room and looked at his watch. It was 0624. The gun crew was already assembling and putting on their big steel helmets.

He counted heads. One man missing.

"Where's Billy Ford?" he asked the gun captain, Gunner's Mate Bart Kendle, the big man the crew called, "Butch."

"In the head, sir," Braddock answered for him,

punctuating his statement with a gesture suggesting masturbation. Then he offered Charlie his usual insolent smile.

Of all the luck, to have that man on his gun crew.

Look at you, a big shot officer, Charlie imagined him saying. *Naval Academy class of '40, all that schooling, and you don't know your ass from an elbow on this boat. You'll probably crap yourself at the first depth charging.*

"Deep six the comedy, Braddock. Butch, get your man."

"There he is, Mr. Harrison."

Billy Ford turned up red-faced. "I'm here! I'm here!"

"Listen, men. The exec wants us to go up top, fire three shells, and secure the gun and all ammunition within the next six minutes. And we're going to do it. Now move."

Butch led his men up the hatch. Another sailor approached Charlie. "We've opened the ammo locker, Mr. Harrison. How many shells should we pass up to the gun crew?"

"Three," Charlie said and followed the crew up the hatch.

They hustled onto the deck. The sun had broken over the horizon, setting the water alight in a fiery orange glare. The men expertly unlimbered the four-inch gun. Butch removed the plug from the barrel and the hinged cover from the loading breech. He inspected the bore to make sure it wasn't obstructed. Charlie checked his work. It was good.

He was starting to take a liking to Butch. The big homely man took his duties seriously and had the gun crew running like a clock. Looking at him, it was hard to believe he was a talented artist and painted with watercolors.

The gun hatch opened on the main deck. A sailor passed up the first cartridge. Charlie checked to make sure it was set to SAFE. All it took was one man dropping a live shell to create a catastrophe.

Then he glanced at his watch. Five minutes. He hustled back to the bridge.

The deck gun had a four-inch bore and was seventeen feet long. Pedestal mounted, it could be rotated by the trainer sitting in the gun's right-hand seat. The pointer, sitting on the other side, controlled the gun barrel's elevation.

Assuming a relatively calm sea, the gun could hit a target far away with decent accuracy and hit it hard. In rougher seas, the swaying of the boat and the length of the barrel made that job harder. Overall, against a merchant or patrol boat, the four-inch gun was an effective weapon.

Against destroyers, it was a Hail Mary.

Which was the point of the exercise. Speed was survival. If a destroyer forced the boat to surface, Frankie would have to hit first, hit hard, and then make a run for it.

"Where's the target?" Butch was asking.

"What?" Charlie called back from the bridge.

"What are we shooting at?"

"Target is 800 yards off the starboard bow!"

Using hand wheels, the trainer turned the gun. The pointer elevated it. The sight setter stood behind the pointer and confirmed the elevation. One of the ammunition handlers stood behind the gun, ready to catch the case as it ejected after firing so he could return it to the magazine.

"You, there!" Charlie racked his brain for the sailor's

53

name. "Borkowski! Where are your gloves?"

The shell case came out hot. The man was supposed to catch it wearing asbestos gloves.

"Forgot them, sir. Sorry, sir."

"Everybody, give him your shirts! Proceed!"

The men removed their T-shirts and handed them over.

The second loader took the first shell from the ammunition train, adjusted it from SAFE to ARMED with a wrench, and handed it to Braddock, the first loader.

"Load," Butch barked.

Braddock rammed the shell into the breech and slammed the block shut. "Ready!"

"Braddock!" Charlie said. "The next time you operate that gun, remember to set the safety."

As first loader, the man was supposed to set the safety so the gun didn't fire accidentally while any crew members were behind the breech. He then removed it before firing.

Braddock waved. "Sorry!" He added quietly in a Japanese accent, "Mr. *Hara-kiri-san*."

The men turned away to hide their grins.

Charlie eyed him, stretching out the time. "Butch, please inform the men they now have two minutes to get their heads out of their ass, fire, secure the weapon, and get back down the hatch. If they fail, on the next field day, they'll be cleaning the boat solo."

The gun captain glared at Braddock. "Straighten up, you asshole."

"Commence firing," Charlie said.

"Fire!" Butch roared.

The boat rocked at the discharge. A wave of smoke shrouded the deck and dissipated in the dawn breeze. Borkowski, his hands wrapped in T-shirts, caught the hot casing.

"Load!"

Braddock accepted the next live shell, shoved it into the breech, and slammed the block. "Ready!"

"Fire!"

The pointer stomped his foot pedal, which fired the gun with another deafening roar. The shell plunged into the Coral Sea with a terrific geyser.

Then the third shot. Another soaring geyser.

"Cease firing!" Charlie ordered. "Secure the gun. Take the casings back to the arsenal."

The men hustled to put the gun back into position and secure it. Charlie observed their movements carefully to ensure the barrel was plugged and the breech covered properly.

Sixty seconds.

"Clear the topsides! Move it!" As Butch passed, he said, "Good handling."

"I do my best with 'em, Mr. Harrison."

They dropped down the hatch and into the control room.

"Butch," Charlie said.

"Sir?"

"With the captain's permission, I'd like to do it again tomorrow, and this time without any screw-ups. What's your best time on the gun?"

"Honestly? I'm pretty sure we beat it today."

"We'll do even better tomorrow. I want the first shell fired within twenty seconds of hitting the deck. We'll drill setting up a few times before we fire the gun."

Butch smiled at the challenge. He gave Charlie a thumbs up.

Charlie returned to the wardroom, where a hot breakfast sat ready for him.

The captain pulled his pipe from his mouth and guffawed. "Nothing like a little early morning exercise to get the blood pumping, eh, Harrison?"

Reynolds, drinking his coffee, said nothing. Nothing needed saying. Charlie hadn't done anything special. He'd done his job, as Reynolds had expected.

The exec stood. "I'll dive the boat. Harrison, when you're done eating, report to the control room and take periscope watch."

"Aye, aye," Charlie answered.

Then he smiled and dug into his bacon and eggs.

CHAPTER TEN

LANDFALL

Charlie sat in a lawn chair in the control room while the S-55 continued to cruise north toward Guadalcanal and Savo Island. More watch duty, this time submerged at a depth of eighty feet, with periodic looks at periscope depth. More tedium, particularly with calm seas.

As the S-55 neared the equator, the boat had grown even hotter. Today, air temperature had risen steadily to ninety degrees. Humidity, nearly 100 percent. Despite the constant effort of high-speed fans, the atmosphere in the boat was stifling.

Charlie looked at the men occupying their stations. After just five days at sea, they looked more like pirates than the Navy's finest. They'd stripped down to shorts and even skivvies. They wore leather sandals. Their pale torsos glistened with sweat. Some had tied skivvy shirts around their necks to absorb their perspiration, which they wrung out into buckets. Their faces bristled with stubble. A planesman had a small prickly heat rash on his back, which, as with everything else, he endured with his breed's peculiar fatalism.

On the S-55, one couldn't tell the officers from the enlisted. Nobody wore insignia while at sea. Only the chiefs wore hats as a sign of status. On his first day on the boat, Charlie had given up wearing his peaked cap; with all the machinery jutting into the work spaces, it was a hazard. On his destroyer, the officers sometimes acted like lords of the manor; here, the crew worked as a team.

And they stank. The boat stank. Frankie's crew drank the water they'd brought, and they washed minimally and shaved even less. Every drop produced by the electric still went to feed the thirsty battery. Boxes of food occupied the boat's only two shower stalls. The thick air reeked of diesel, body odor, cigarette smoke, and cooking smells—right now, chicken frying in the galley. The hull ventilation carried these mingled odors throughout the boat.

Towels littered the floor to catch water that condensed and dripped down the cool bulkhead walls. Cockroaches, which were making a comeback, rustled happily in their folds.

A hell of a way to fight a war, indeed.

Sweat dripped off Charlie's nose and onto his chest. His mind drifted as the ever-present hum of machinery lulled him into a brief doze. The sea was calm today, so there was nothing to do on periscope watch except wait until it was time to take another look at the surface.

The Army had a reputation for being hurry-up-and-wait. Fighting a war in a submarine was turning out to be wait-and-hurry-up, and he was still waiting.

Rusty entered the control room and handed Charlie a pair

of salt tablets and a bottle of cold lemonade. "You wouldn't happen to have any medical training or know-how, would you?"

"No more than you," Charlie told him.

The 55 didn't have any medical staff. If a man got wounded by enemy action or working with the sub's machinery, caught appendicitis, or needed a tooth pulled, he went to Rusty.

The lieutenant sighed. "Then I guess I'll keep the job. If you'll excuse me, I've got to go treat two sexy sailors who caught the clap in Brisbane. Hooray for me."

Charlie nodded, too exhausted by the heat to respond to Rusty's banter. He swallowed the salt pills, which he hoped would revive his flagging energy, and chugged half the cold lemonade with a contented sigh. Then he noticed the time.

"Planes, forty-five feet," he said.

The boat angled up and held steady at periscope depth.

He pushed himself up from his chair. "Up scope." He crouched, pulled the handles down, and followed the scope as it rose. Cool seawater rained on him from the upper bearings. Mercifully, the optic wasn't fogged; an auxiliaryman had applied a desiccant that absorbed the moisture. But the scope vibrated, making seeing anything an irritating challenge.

The placid sea was smooth as a sheet of glass that gleamed under a tropical sun. Even with only a foot of periscope showing above the water and the boat moving at a slow speed, he was likely leaving an easily detectable feather in the water. Something a passing anti-submarine warfare plane could zero in on; he'd have to make this quick. He swung the periscope 360 degrees, scanning the sea and the sky above it. Empty.

"All clear," he said. "Down scope. Planes, eighty feet."

He felt like he was finally getting the hang of this, that he was starting to become a part of it.

He climbed into the conning tower, where the air was slightly cooler, and looked out the glass portholes. Even at eighty feet, he could clearly see schools of colorful fish swim past. No wonder the submariners called the sea the "fish tank," and the boat a "people tank." The fish were beautiful; he wondered what they thought of him.

He descended into the control room and slumped in the lawn chair. His lemonade had gone warm. Ten minutes until the next look up top. To pass the time, he asked the men what it was like at Cavite during the bombing. They eagerly took to the subject.

"Pearl had already been hit," the bow planesman said. "We were on alert. We knew we were in for it. We'd lost our air cover. The Japs could hit us at will."

"And they did," Donatelli, the hydraulic manifoldman, chimed in. "I remember it like it was yesterday. Fifty Jap bombers breaking into two neat formations, then five. So far up, just little contrails in the sky. No evasive action. Arrogant sons of bitches. They took their time. We were all standing around pointing up at them. I couldn't believe it was happening."

Then they were all talking over each other in their excitement.

"Our ack-acks threw a lot of lead into the sky—"

"You could see the tracers reaching for the planes, but they were out of range—"

"Might as well have been shooting at the clouds—"

"Then the bombs hit—"

"And the fucking Japs slaughtered us—"

While the air raid sirens wailed, bombs whistled onto Cavite by the ton, bringing Armageddon. The earth shook with cataclysmic detonations as the docks blew apart and turned the navy yard into a hellish inferno. The barracks flattened; the machine shop blazed. The torpedo plant exploded, flinging deadly shrapnel. A big oil tank went up in a blinding flash. The sky blackened with thick, rolling clouds of smoke.

Men screamed and ran for cover or fought the flames. The *Bittern* was on fire, the *Sealion* smashed by multiple hits and sinking by the stern, the *Seadragon* and the S-55 riddled with jagged holes. The S-55 settled on the bottom, only showing its smoking metal sail, which convinced the Japs she was sunk. The Japanese bombers swept overhead again and again, in no rush, methodically checking that their targets were destroyed and dropping more bombs if they weren't. More than a thousand dockworkers died, mostly Filipinos.

"This boat lost a few good men too," Donatelli said. "Three, to be exact."

The men remembered their dead comrades in silence. Then they started up again.

Charlie listened with wide-eyed fascination as they told their stories of horror and heroism in a matter-of-fact manner. After a while, he remembered to check the clock.

"Time for another look up top," he said. "Planes, forty-five feet." Once the boat had leveled off at periscope depth, he added, "Up scope."

He scanned the skies and saw the distant dot of a plane.

"Plane, far, bearing oh-nine-five, elevation four-triple-oh, crossing the bow." No threat.

Then he saw the smudge on the horizon. Land.

"Inform the captain we've made landfall," Charlie told the yeoman. "You may tell him we've reached Guadalcanal."

Guadalcanal, the battleground of the Eastern Solomons.

He smiled. They'd reach their patrol station at Savo Island by the end of the day. They'd be in the St. George Channel tonight, in the dark, when the Japanese came down the Slot. He was a part of this now. He was about to get into the fight.

Charlie had a strong feeling that, by the end of this patrol, he'd have his own stories to tell.

CHAPTER ELEVEN
PATROL STATION

Rigged for red. Ready to surface in all respects. The surfacing alarm sounding.

The S-55 gently broke the surface of Savo Sound, the ocean inlet the men of the beleaguered Pacific Fleet were calling Iron Bottom Sound after numerous sharp naval battles.

Ready for the first night watch, Charlie held the ladder tightly as the hatch partly opened. A heavy blast of sour air roared past him.

After the air pressure equalized and the tempest subsided, he climbed up and looked around. It was a routine to which he'd already become accustomed, but he felt a special urgency about it now.

They were in the Slot, and they'd received a message to expect a Japanese naval force passing through the area later tonight. After days of seeing no enemy ships, it was exciting news.

He took his time and scanned the area thoroughly. Aided by the budding moon, his night-adapted eyes picked out Savo Island to the east, Guadalcanal to the south.

"All clear," he called down. "Lookouts to the bridge."

Steam drifted out of the open hatch. His men emerged and took their stations.

Charlie took a deep breath of the clean air and inhaled the vital scent of jungle wafting from the nearby islands. After a day in the people tank, it smelled sweeter than Evie's perfume. The temperature was considerably cooler topside at seventy-five degrees.

The main induction opened to suck the cool night air into the boat for both the crew and the engines. The diesels fired up to charge the battery while the boat stood-to facing north by west. By the end of Charlie's watch, the battery had fully charged, and both diesels were assigned to the propellers. The old sea wolf was ready to hunt.

Rusty mounted to the bridge. "Permission to relieve you and your squires, noble sir. As incentive for that permission, I can tell you a sumptuous meal awaits you in the wardroom."

"In that case, permission granted," Charlie said. "What's the cook serving up for dinner?"

"Pot roast and cock, and he's all out of pot roast."

Charlie laughed. Ever since the S-55 entered the Solomons, the men had stopped their shirking and horsing around and went to work with silent efficiency. But not Rusty. Not even the tension of imminent combat could keep the able lieutenant from his wisecracks.

Kidding aside, despite the hardships of service, submariners ate better than anybody else in the Navy, at least while the fresh provisions lasted. Right now, pot roast sounded fantastic.

"All sectors clear," he told Rusty. "A dozen lighted planes, far off and coming across the stern, were reported. Navy fighters landing at Henderson Field."

"Hopefully, they bombed those tin cans headed our way."

"We should be so lucky," Charlie agreed, though he was itching for a fight.

As the new watch manned their stations, he descended the stairs to the cigarette deck and then the main deck. He tied a metal bucket to a manila rope, tossed it over the side, and pulled up cool seawater. Then he started a quick sponge bath.

For a war zone, the scene struck him as peaceful. The slim moon's light glimmered on the water, which lapped gently against the boat's hull. His romantic Evie would have loved it.

He heard a distant droning and perked up. He hustled back to the bridge while the watch scanned the skies.

A burst of light flared in the distance and died out. Then another. Moments later, he heard the first boom. Red tracers streamed into the night.

"Ho-lee shit," one of the watchmen said.

More bright flashes brightened the horizon. The air filled with thunder and the distant wail of an air raid siren. Searchlights swept the sky.

The Japanese were bombing the airfield on Guadalcanal.

"Lookouts, get below," somebody shouted up the shaft. "Clear the bridge!"

Bodies poured down the hatch. Charlie dropped to the

deck and jumped out of the way. One by one, the rest of the men came down after him, talking excitedly.

"Hatch secured!" Rusty called from above.

The captain said, "Dive, dive, dive!"

The diving alarm sounded. The main induction clanged shut.

"Pressure in the boat, green board," Reynolds reported. The boat was sealed up tight.

The S-55 rapidly slid into the black waters and achieved a good trim at periscope depth. The engines cut out. The electric motors engaged the propellers.

"Planes, forty-five feet."

"What's going on?" Charlie asked Rusty.

The lieutenant shrugged. "The captain pulled the plug."

"Silence!" Kane roared, quieting them all.

The men stared at the captain. The captain stared at the soundman.

"I've got a turn count of 325 RPM," Marsh said. "Now I'm hearing multiple sets of screws. Light screws. Speed estimated twenty-five knots."

Charlie grinned. That sounded like destroyers!

Marsh added, "Estimated range, 8,000 yards."

The captain put on his sou'wester hat and oilskins. "Up scope."

He peered into the dark, whistling a popular tune while water splashed on his shoulders. "Give me a bearing, Marsh."

"Targets, bearing one-one-five." Plus or minus a few degrees.

The submarine's Great War-vintage hydrophones weren't perfectly accurate, but one thing was certain: The Japanese war party was coming straight at them. They intended to round Savo Island. Charlie guessed their mission was to give Henderson a good shelling tonight.

The captain smiled as he looked into the scope. "I think I see them. Come to papa. Down scope. Harrison, start plotting. Marsh, keep those bearings coming."

Charlie dumped graph paper, pencils, and a ruler onto the plotting table. He marked the contacts' estimated position.

"Bearing still on one-one-five."

Based on the war party's bearing and estimated speed, he marked its likely new position on the plotting paper. He checked the boat's gyrocompass and started plotting the S-55's relative position with a pencil and ruler.

"Left full rudder," the captain said. "All ahead full. Come right to two-seven-five." After the heavy sub completed her ponderous turn and found her new course, he added, "All ahead one-third. Up scope." After another look at the approaching ships: "Down scope."

Deep in thought, Captain Kane stepped away from the falling periscope.

He had a choice. He could take a shot at the destroyers as they passed and then radio their presence to warn American forces at Guadalcanal they were coming. Or he could let them pass, sound the alarm, and try to hit them on their way back.

Both carried risks. The former approach put them directly in a hornet's nest. The latter was safer, but the Japanese might take another route home, and Frankie would miss her chance to take a crack at them.

Knowing the captain, Charlie believed he'd take the latter, more cautious approach.

Kane rubbed his stubbled jaw. The men stared at him, awaiting his command.

"Battle stations," he said. "Torpedo attack."

CHAPTER TWELVE
THE DESTROYERS

The battle stations alarm bonged throughout the boat.

"Battle stations, torpedo," the quartermaster announced over the 1MC.

Around the S-55, all hands scrambled to man their stations for the attack.

In the control room, Reynolds would act as assistant approach officer and Rusty as assistant diving officer. Charlie remained on station as plotting officer.

The submarine started an attack approach, cruising toward the enemy ships at a new submerged depth of seventy feet. Going in slow and deep while raising the periscope as little as possible.

"All compartments report battle stations manned," the telephone talker reported.

Charlie felt his first pangs of fear. He'd served on a destroyer. He knew how good they were at fighting submarines. In fact, the destroyer was the submarine's natural enemy. Fast and nimble. Bristling with sonar, big guns, and depth charges.

The S-55 taking on these powerful ships was David and

Goliath all over again. Though, in this case, David carried a pretty big stone.

The soundman called out a new bearing. Charlie forgot his fear as he marked positions on the plotting paper. He had a job to do. Lives depended on him right now, just as they depended on every other man on the boat.

Five minutes passed. Five more. Wait and hurry up. In the dim red light of the control room, the dots and lines on the paper showed the Japanese ships and the S-55 slowly converging.

"They're zigging," the soundman reported.

To avoid a surprise submarine attack, destroyers often zigzagged, but they commonly did so based on a pattern. Charlie marked the new bearing and used his ruler to draw a straight line between the last two dots. After a few plots, the pattern would emerge. Then Frankie could get into a final position to take a shot at them.

"Steady as she goes," Kane said. The cat and mouse game was on in earnest now.

The captain studied the plot Charlie built mark by mark. The approach was an exercise in geometry. Kane had to maneuver his moving object to be at the precise place to shoot at objects that were themselves moving.

Frankie's luck held. The Japanese ships came on as neatly as if she'd laid a trap. After turning the boat to starboard on a new northerly course of zero-one-zero, Captain Kane nudged her toward a firing position.

Rusty had been right; the man's hands didn't shake in combat. A cool customer.

The young officer tracking a target while Kane, hands on his hips, stood over him; it was like doing a classroom problem at Submarine School. Fear of failure, not of dying.

The captain tapped the paper with his finger. *There. That's where we'll take a shot at the bastards*. Charlie envisioned the attack. The enemy ships would present their broadsides as they passed at between 1,000 and 1,500 yards. Frankie would be on course to lead her target by twenty-nine degrees—speed plus three—for a straight bow shot. Beautiful.

The captain brought the boat to forty-five feet. "Up scope."

He whistled again as he scanned the darkness. "I can see them clearly now in the moonlight. Three *Fubuki*-class destroyers. And what looks like a heavy cruiser. I think it's the *Furutaka*. A *Furutaka*-class cruiser, just like the *Kako*, which the 44 sank around these parts back in August."

The men in the control room glanced at each other and grinned.

The captain said, "Nine thousand tons. That's the ship we're going to sink."

He spoke with a light tone that betrayed nothing of the mounting pressure he must have felt. In fact, he sounded positively delighted at the prospect of taking a shot at the giant.

Then he brought the boat down to seventy feet, staying hidden.

"Rig for depth charge," he said.

Around the boat, men prepared the boat to take a beating. All unnecessary lights were extinguished and emergency lighting turned on. Watertight doors banged shut.

With three destroyers up top, the captain was expecting swift and severe retaliation after Frankie sent the *Furutaka* to the bottom.

"All compartments report rigged for depth charge," the telephone talker said.

"Very well."

Rusty murmured to Charlie, "Having fun?"

Charlie wasn't sure how a professional should answer that one. He decided to be honest. "Hell, yeah."

"This part always is."

"Helm, steer oh-oh-five," the captain said, nudging their course. He brought the boat back up for forty-five feet again. "Up scope. We're getting close."

The excitement in the room was almost palpable now.

Charlie spared a moment of reflection for their strangely methodical and deadly work. The men turned wheels, pushed buttons, pulled levers, studied instrumentation. At the end of this highly technical process, a hole would be blown in a big ship, and it would sink into the sound.

Possibly hundreds of men would be killed.

He wondered about those men out there. The Japanese remained an alien race to him, but they weren't evil or inhuman. They loved their children. They toiled on the same types of ships. They laughed. They dreamed. They suffered, and they died, just like any man.

In the end, none of it mattered. The Japanese slaughtered thousands at Pearl. More than a thousand at Cavite. While the individual Japanese wasn't so different from Charlie, he served a brutal regime that enslaved millions and threatened America.

Rusty was fighting for his wife and son. Charlie fought for Evie, but more than Evie, he was fighting for his country. The people in it and, just as important, the very idea of it.

The captain read the periscope's stadimeter. "Range, 1,500 yards. It's show time. Torpedo room, make ready the tubes. Order of tubes is one, two, three, four. Set depth at four feet."

In the torpedo compartment, the sailors loaded the torpedoes. The tubes flooded. The outer doors opened.

"All four tubes ready, Captain," Reynolds confirmed.

"Torpedo room, stand by."

The seconds ticked by. Charlie gaped at the captain, pencil clenched in his hand. Kane stared into the scope for another minute while water splashed on his bare shoulders.

"He's coming on. Easy does it. Fire one!"

Reynolds punched the firing button. "Firing one."

Frankie shuddered as the torpedo ejected from its tube, a ton of metal and explosives suddenly exiting the boat.

Reynolds counted eight seconds on his stopwatch and pressed the plunger for the second tube. "Firing two!"

Another eight seconds: "Firing three!"

Then: "Firing four! Secure all tubes."

Four torpedoes in a longitudinal spread. If all went according to plan, the first torpedo would hit the cruiser close to the bow. The ship's momentum would carry it forward, allowing the other fish to nail her both amidships and near the stern. As the cruiser was nearly six football fields in length, the odds looked good.

The torpedoes streamed in a single line toward the cruiser. At this range, nearly two minutes would pass before the contact-exploders struck the hull and detonated.

This was it. Charlie's heart pounded. He took a deep breath to steady himself.

"Hell," Kane said, his eyes glued to the scope. His hands tightened their grip on the handles. "Our first fish is going erratic. Doing a crazy sine wave to port."

The defective torpedo was leaving a luminescent wake and heading directly at the destroyers. By making a pattern, it practically screamed for attention.

The captain said, "They're breaking formation. They spotted the torpedo. They're scattering. *Furutaka* is turning toward us. Our other three fish are going to miss along her port side." He vented his frustration with a sigh. "Now they're—"

He turned from the scope. "Dive, dive, dive! Take her deep, emergency!"

CHAPTER THIRTEEN
COUNTERATTACK

Crash dive. The diving alarm sounding.

The S-55 plunged into the depths. The deck tilted steeply. Charlie grabbed a handhold as the pencils rolled off the plotting table.

"Take her down," the captain said. "Right full rudder! All ahead flank!"

"Passing eighty feet," Rusty reported. The electric motors gave everything they had to deliver maximum speed.

"The lead destroyer was coming on fast with a bone in his teeth," Kane said. In other words, showing a pronounced bow wake. "That Jap skipper was trying to ram us."

Charlie already heard the warship approaching on fast screws.

Rusty, paling, looked at Charlie. "We're in for it now."

whoosh whoosh whoosh whoosh

The destroyer was passing overhead. The men shot anxious looks at the overhead bulkhead and grabbed the nearest handholds.

WHAAAMMM

The explosion shook the boat. A light bulb burst, spraying

glass. Dust drifted down from cork insulation on the bulkheads. The big machines vibrated in their mountings.

The depth charges were drums packed with 200 pounds of explosives more powerful than TNT. Within fifty feet, the submarine took a beating. Within twenty-five feet, an explosion was likely to sink her. Water hammer cracked the hull like an egg.

The clicking sound was the detonator. Charlie knew that when you heard the click, the depth charge was close aboard.

"Knife to a gunfight," Reynolds said with disgust.

click

WHAAAMMM, WHAAAMMM, WHAAAMMM

Charlie's feet left the floor. Men were tossed to the deck. Gauge glasses and light bulbs shattered. Cork insulation burst into the air, and Charlie felt something strike his face. He touched his stinging cheek. His fingers came away bloody.

"That's a Purple Heart," Rusty said. His face was white as a sheet. "I told you you'd go far in the Navy."

The planesmen fought to keep control of the boat. Across the sealed compartment, men coughed on the dust. The dust and feeble lighting shrouded Charlie's vision in red. Marsh threw up in a bucket.

Rusty reported, "Final trim, 150 feet."

"All compartments, rig for silent running and report leaks." The captain glanced up and frowned as the ghostly ring of short-scale pinging filled the boat. "That was a good ass whipping, but they're not done with us yet."

The telephone talker passed on the message to all

compartments. The ventilation blowers and refrigerator motors were turned off. The helm and bow and stern planes switched to manual control. All nonessential personnel hurried to their bunks.

From now on, Frankie would make very little noise for the enemy sonar to find.

"We're trimmed heavy," Reynolds said. "We're taking water."

The telephone talker said, "Engine compartment reports a blown hatch gasket."

Charlie glanced at the Christmas Tree, a row of indicator lights that should have all been green, indicating the boat's hatches were sealed up tight. One glared bright red.

That was bad, Charlie knew. Water was gushing into the sealed room, and nobody could do a damned thing about it until they got back to the surface. *If* they got back.

He gaped up at the bulkhead, waiting.

The destroyers' screws speeded up as the ships straddled the suspected location of the S-55.

whoosh whoosh whoosh whoosh

Then he laughed quietly at the absurdity of it all.

"Are you nuts?" Rusty asked him.

"I was just thinking—"

click-WHAAAMMM

The thunder of multiple explosions slammed the boat. The world's biggest hammer pounded the S-55's hull like a gong. The destroyers had dropped two patterns of seven depth charges on the submariners' heads.

The boat tilted. She was sinking by the bow.

"Put a bubble in the number one main ballast tank," Kane ordered.

The manifoldman injected a shot of high-pressure air into the main ballast tank, which should have checked their slide. But the boat continued to sink.

Charlie gripped his handhold. How close was the S-55 to her test depth?

WHAAAMMM

WHAAAMMM

WHAAAMMM

The concussions shook the piping. Instruments shattered. Chunks of cork whirled across the compartment in fresh clouds of dust. A tiny high-pressure stream of seawater shot from a break in a weld in the conning tower. Then another.

"Put another bubble in the tank!"

The boat should have responded. Something was wrong. The hull might have been cracked in one of the forward compartments, flooding it and dragging the boat down.

If that was true, they were all in big trouble.

"Passing 160 feet, Captain!" Rusty said.

Above the S-55's test depth, but lower than she was typically expected to handle.

Charlie scanned the diving board. A red indicator light caught his eye. The number one main ballast tank's vent had been left open during the preparations for the depth charging. Every time the manifoldman shot more air into the tank, it passed straight through.

The air then shot up to the surface as a big popping bubble, a beacon alerting the Japanese destroyers to their exact position.

"Captain, the vent's open!" he said.

"Shut the vent on the tank and give me another bubble," Kane told the manifoldman.

The air entered the tank and checked the boat's descent.

It took Charlie another moment to realize the worst of the attack was over, leaving a loud ringing in his ears. The last booms of the depth charges sounded astern. The speeding-train churn of the destroyers' screws faded to the southeast. Then a set of heavier screws thrashed overhead as the cruiser passed.

"Lucky for us they have a schedule to keep," Rusty gasped. "Giving somebody else hell."

A light rain fell in the control room. Broken glass littered the deck. Filthy water puddled at their feet. The place was a disaster.

"Secure from depth charge," the captain said. "Secure from battle stations."

"No power, sir," the stern planesman grunted. "We're barely keeping her afloat on an even keel." After fifteen minutes of working the helm and planes manually, they were exhausted.

"Get me replacements to relieve these men," Kane said. "Ten-minute shifts. Rig to surface. And inform all compartments I expect a detailed damage report. Reynolds, on surfacing, you'll be OOD. I'm going with Rusty to evaluate the damage and prioritize repairs."

"Aye, aye, Captain," the exec said. He had a bruise on his face and a cut on his forehead.

"Orders, Captain?" Charlie said.

"After we surface, radio Perth so they can warn Guadalcanal that they've got some heavy-hitting tin cans headed their way. Then you'll help Reynolds with running the boat and us with repairs as needed. But before you do that, I have a small but important job for you."

"What's that, sir?"

"Splice the mainbrace," Rusty cut in. He smiled a grim smile. In the harsh emergency lighting, he looked like an old man again. "Starting with me, if you don't mind."

The Navy had been dry since 1912, but submarines carried medicinal brandy in small bottles to hand out after severe depth charging. His task was to brace the crew, assuming the bottles survived the attack. Charlie decided he could stand a little bracing himself. Once the attack started, he'd stopped being scared. The thought he might die never crossed his mind.

Now that it was over, he tingled with shock. He leaned against the table, unsure whether he could stand on legs that had turned to rubber.

"Aye, aye, sir."

"So what were you thinking?" Rusty asked him. "When you laughed like a madman? Emperor Hirohito's A-team rudely cut you off before you could tell me."

"What? Oh, it's not important. I was just thinking, 'Evie's going to be furious with me.'"

Rusty barked a short laugh. "If I were you, I'd leave this little incident out of your next letter. Now let's see if we can make it back to the surface so you can send it."

CHAPTER FOURTEEN

DAMAGE REPORT

Back on the surface, the men toiled on the S-55 to keep her seaworthy.

They were out of danger, but not out of trouble. They had to submerge before daylight, when the sky would become dotted with enemy planes.

First, they had a lot of repairs to perform.

Charlie wrote a message by the light of a shielded flashlight and handed it to Marsh. When the S-55 was submerged, he was a soundman. On the surface, he acted as radioman.

"My ears are still ringing," Marsh said, wiggling his pinkie in his ear.

Charlie's were as well. "Send this to Perth immediately."

"Aye, aye, Mr. Harrison." Marsh retreated to the radio room.

The telephone talker said, "Bridge, stay clear of the antennae. We're transmitting."

Time to distribute the "depth charge medicine" to the crew.

All compartments abaft of the control room had gone

dark except for emergency lighting and hand lanterns, the result of a failed lighting circuit. Two electrician's mates in the aft repair party directed their flashlights at an auxiliary power board.

"Try it now," the shorter one said.

The circuit breaker hissed and spit sparks. They turned it off.

The man said, "You disconnected the wrong one, Mac. *That's* the one. The one that's *wet*. Good. Now throw the switch."

Much to Charlie's relief, the lights came back on as he passed them.

He was still processing the night's events. Overall, the S-55 and her crew had performed commendably, particularly the captain, who'd conned the boat into an ideal firing position and kept his head during the battle. But one of the Great War-vintage torpedoes had blown the attack.

It would have been something to sink a cruiser on his first patrol. Instead, he came close to becoming a permanent resident of the bottom, one of the war's many footnotes.

Charlie took stock of his reactions to the battle. Strange how he hadn't felt much fear until after it was all over. He'd been too busy, too focused. And he'd kept his head the entire time. He was able to not only endure the depth charging but think and act coolly and rationally during it. It was only afterward that his mind blanked out and his legs turned to jelly.

Splice the mainbrace, aye. He needed a shot of the old medicine himself.

He unlocked the pharmacy locker and filled three buckets with the little bottles of medicinal brandy, which he handed out to the crew as he worked his way forward. Being the bearer of a stiff drink, he enjoyed a taste of being the most popular man on the boat.

Working his way forward, he visited the crew berths, where he knew he'd find casualties. A torpedoman had the shakes bad. A messmate lay on his bunk in wide-eyed shock. A third man grimaced over splints hastily applied to three fingers on his left hand.

He helped the first two take a drink and gave the third a double ration.

In the passageway, a gruff voice: "Hey, you forgot about me."

Charlie turned as Braddock approached, his muscular torso splattered with oil.

"I don't see how I could have missed you, Braddock. Your presence calls attention to itself."

The machinist twisted off the cap and downed the liquor. He winked. "Thank *you*, sir."

Then he tramped off to repair his machines and save the boat again.

The man had winked. A peace offering? Whatever it was, it was a start. Rusty was right about one thing. These guys were jerks *and* heroes.

Returning aft, he found the lieutenant ankle deep in brackish water in the engine compartment. He handed him his bottle.

"Buddy, you're a dream," Rusty said. He tossed back the

brandy and sighed at the empty bottle. "Now I can face this shit."

"How bad is it?"

"We got that gasket repaired and patched the worst breaks in the welds, so at least we're not taking water faster than the pumps can push it out of the boat. We're soap-testing the main induction for a leak. We've got grounds in the battery to clear out and a sluggish air compressor to troubleshoot. After that, we can look forward to an hour or two splicing and wrapping new wiring in the starboard main motor after a grounded wire caused a fire."

Charlie couldn't help but laugh. "Is that it?"

Rusty smiled back. "Give me a chance. I've only had time for a quick look at everything. This is the kind of boat where, the more you look, the more you find."

"Anything I can do to help?"

"Yeah. Get that cut on your face squared away."

"I will."

Rusty gave him a knowing stare. "You might need stitches, Charlie. Some women adore ugly scars, but most don't. And you don't need a nasty infection keeping you from duty. Clean it, and if it's deep, put some tape over it until I can stitch you up. I'm serious."

Rusty, being serious? "All right," he said, meaning it this time.

"Then go see if Reynolds needs you. If he doesn't, I've got plenty of work for you and every other swinging dick on this boat. Remember, we may be sailors on this sugar boat, but we're mechanics first."

Charlie went to the mess room, where the cook and his mates laid out trays of sandwiches for the crew. He handed out the rest of the liquor and inspected his face in the reflection of a cooking pot. It was a mess. He cleaned up with a wet rag. Thankfully, he didn't need stitches. He admired his shaggy appearance. With his unkempt hair and budding beard, he was starting to look like a mountain man. If only Evie could see him now!

He poured some hydrogen peroxide over his cuts, which stung and sizzled. He taped a bandage over them. He pocketed the last bottle of brandy, which he was keeping for himself.

On his return to the control room, Reynolds fixed him with a burning glare, no doubt missing his nicotine. It didn't take him long to figure out the real reason the exec was smoldering.

Hirohito's finest had given Frankie a real beating. The damage she'd taken might require Kane to abort the mission and return to Brisbane for tender work. Frankie could be out of the war for days, weeks, maybe even months.

As far as combat patrols went, this one was turning into a real dud.

"I'd like to clean up that cut on your head, if you don't mind," he said.

"Get lost," Reynolds said. "There's plenty other work for you."

Somehow, he didn't think the exec would respond to the same tough love that Rusty had given him about his own cuts.

"Aye, aye," he said and thought, *Getting lost, aye, sir.*

Marsh told him the radio message had gotten out, but the boat wasn't receiving. As a result, the radioman couldn't confirm receipt of the message or answer base calls.

An emergency repair party stopped up the holes in the conning tower with plugs and were now reinforcing them with wood planks. Charlie and Marsh climbed past the men to the bridge to have a look at the radio receiver.

Frankie lay hove-to. Bits and pieces of the exploded depth charges floated on the sea. Shrapnel littered the bridge. Sailors dumped trash cans of garbage and filthy water into the drink. A growing oil slick bloomed astern, the result of the pumps working hard to empty the bilges out to sea.

Booms to the south. Flashes along the horizon. The lookouts pointed.

The Japanese raiding party had opened up with their six- and eight-inch guns at the Marines on Guadalcanal. The Marines were catching hell.

"I hope Perth relayed the message to warn those guys," Marsh said.

"If they sent their planes after them, they don't seem to be having much of an effect."

The radioman looked pale in the weak moonlight. "Mr. Harrison?"

"What's wrong?"

"What if those ships return the same way they came?"

Charlie smiled. "We'd better hurry up with these repairs." He added, "If the destroyers come back, we'll hightail it, and they'll see all this garbage and think they sank us."

Though, he doubted the Japanese would come back this way now that they knew a submarine was operating in the area.

They completed their work and returned to the control room. Reynolds told him to have a look at the number one periscope. The exec had tested it, and it had stuck in train.

"Aye, aye."

Radio music began playing over the loudspeakers. Charlie got to work on the periscope. He found a shard of metal caught in the barrel and removed it. How it got in there was a mystery. The forces unleashed during a depth charge attack tested his knowledge of physics.

"Try it now," Charlie told Reynolds.

The periscope worked, a small victory in the battle to repair the boat.

The song ended. Tokyo Rose began speaking. Her voice was mechanical but also incredibly sultry to the female-starved crew of the S-boat. A Japanese Greta Garbo.

"I have just received the tragic news that an American submarine has been sunk near Guadalcanal."

The men in the control room perked up at that. They stopped their work to listen.

"No better than pirates, they preyed on innocent merchants in defiance of civilized rules of war and international treaties. But the loss of such fine men is a tragedy. Think of those poor grieving mothers and widows. Now think of yourself, sailor. Probably you too will never return to your wife or sweetheart. For what? Why are you so far from your sweet home? It's time to give up. You have fought well, but your war of aggression is futile. Surrender is

honorable."

"I'll surrender if you will, baby," one of the manifoldmen breathed. The man had a crush on the propagandist's husky voice that couldn't be reasoned with.

"Silence," Reynolds snarled. "They sank one of our boats. Who the hell was it?"

Both the S-37 and the S-41 were also operating in the Solomons.

"To the poor departed sailors of the S-55 sunk near Guadalcanal, I will dedicate this next song, which might be appropriate."

The loudspeakers began playing, "Rocked in the Cradle of the Deep."

Across the boat, the men laughed.

Charlie remembered his own spirit ration in his pocket and raised his bottle.

"To the 55," he said and drank.

CHAPTER FIFTEEN

THE EMERGENCY

Charlie awoke with a start.

He'd been awake for nearly thirty hours. Asleep for what felt like minutes.

"—the LTJG!"

"What?" he asked in pure confusion. His heart pounded against his ribs. "What?"

"The boat's still trimmed heavy. I was told to blow the LTJG."

"What? Is that you, Billy?"

"Yes, Mr. Harrison. Please hurry, sir. I was told you know where the LTJG is."

Charlie frowned. LTJG was shorthand for "lieutenant, junior-grade."

Another prank on the two greenhorns.

"Who told you that?"

"Machinist's Mate John Braddock. He said to give you his compliments and to tell you it's an emergency that the LTJG get blown. I'm supposed to do it myself."

"Tell Braddock I said he's an idiot. Tell him I said the LTJG got blown just a few days before we got underway and can't be blown again until his main ballast tanks are full."

Puzzled: "Sir?"

"Tell him what I said, Billy. Word for word. Now get lost so I can sleep."

"Aye, aye." The kid ran off.

Moments later, Charlie heard quiet laughter from Rusty's bunk.

"I'm glad you think it's funny," Charlie growled.

"It's the little things that get you through a war," Rusty chuckled. "The little things."

CHAPTER SIXTEEN
A GAME OF STRATEGY

Charlie awoke with the terrible feeling he'd missed something important.

As his consciousness cleared the cobwebs from his brain, he realized nothing was wrong. He'd simply slept a long time, much longer than the normal six hours a day.

The captain's doing, he suspected. Repairs had been completed. Through superhuman effort, Frankie had been brought back to something resembling fighting trim. Kane was now resting his crew for battles ahead.

Rusty snored in his bunk, dead to the world.

What time was it? Sometime during the day, judging by the heat; he was bathed in sweat. Frankie was submerged. Charlie read his watch. 1537.

He slept as the crew did—in his shorts with a rolled-up pair of dungarees as a pillow. Still feeling groggy, he rolled off his sweat-soaked bunk and slipped his feet into his sandals. He used the officers' head and got a cup of coffee in the wardroom.

Kane dozed in one of the chairs, arms folded across his chest, still holding his pipe. The captain roused and regarded

Charlie with a fatherly smile. "Ready for duty, Harrison?"

Charlie sat and held up his cup of coffee. The oppressive heat normally made him avoid it during submergence, but he needed the boost. The gesture said, *I'll do anything you ask, Captain, but after my coffee.*

Kane smiled. "Make sure you eat something too. Nimuel will bring you a sandwich."

"Thank you, sir."

"Perhaps you feel fit enough for a game of chess while we eat."

Charlie was so used to automatically responding to the captain's wishes with, "Aye, aye," it took him a moment to realize the captain was making a request, not a command.

A game of chess sounded fun; he enjoyed the game, which sharpened the mind. Normally, the officers spent their off-duty hours in card games like Hearts and Bridge. They required strategy too but not nearly as much as chess did, in Charlie's view.

He said, "I'd like that, sir. But maybe you should think about catching up on your own sleep, if you don't mind me saying."

"I'm too tired to sleep. A challenging game will help rest my mind. I hope you're planning to challenge me."

"That's the plan, sir. But we all know what happens to plans."

The captain reached behind him and produced a battered chessboard and box of pieces. He poured out the contents of the box, and he and Charlie began setting up their game.

By privilege of rank, the captain took white. He opened

with the Queen's Gambit. Charlie saw a swift and bloody confrontation over the board's strategically vital central four squares. After another moment's thought, he moved one of his pawns.

Kane lit his pipe and waved the match. "You move quickly. You should think through every decision before moving, no matter how small the stakes. Do you know why?"

"Because I might get sloppy and make a mistake?"

"More than that. It could be a good move. But there might be a better one."

Charlie nodded. The coffee and the game were reviving him. Nimuel brought in some bacon sandwiches and a pitcher of cold water, and he dug into the meal with a hearty appetite.

Kane said, "Friendly forces are moving into Area Roger today. Which means we'll have to stay out of their way. And when we catch a ship, we'll have to try to make contact with the blinker gun first to make sure it's not friendly."

"That doesn't sound very enabling to our advantage of surprise." In fact, it sounded like a great way to get sunk by a salvo of six-inch guns.

"We have little enough of that left anyway, since the enemy now knows submarines are operating around Savo. We've lost the initiative. Important in both war and chess. Check."

He'd timed the move well to prove his point. Charlie countered with his bishop, which now threatened the captain's queen. When the captain withdrew his queen,

Charlie pounced with his bishop. "Your king is in check, sir."

"I see you're a fast learner."

Kane blocked the bishop with his knight. Charlie traded pieces, resulting in the captain doubling up his pawns on the right side of the board. A weakness to be exploited later.

The captain said, "But you're still not thinking things through."

He brought his queen forward to take a pawn, threatening Charlie's rook on his left flank. Charlie's only option was to shift his rook next to his king and let the flank collapse. But the captain's bishop threatened the square next to Charlie's king. His rook was doomed.

A neat little trap. Charlie studied the board carefully now, looking for relief. "So it appears we'll be spending the rest of our patrol staying out of everybody's way."

"Think of the 55's dilemma as a game of chess, Harrison. The enemy has the initiative. He's boxing you in. What do you do?"

"Regain the initiative, of course," Charlie answered. "Counter threat with threat."

"How do you do that?"

"Go somewhere he's weak and doesn't expect you. Decisively and aggressively."

The captain toked on his pipe, releasing a burst of cherry-smelling smoke. "Yes."

Charlie saw the captain's plan now. "We're leaving Area Roger. Moving up the St. George Channel." To Rabaul? No, the captain had made his feelings clear that he didn't want to take that much risk. "Right into the heart of the Slot."

Kane smiled. "Right again. Brisbane approved my request this morning. The 41 will take over Area Roger."

The captain's strategy would put Frankie into a hornet's nest, far from help. But she'd regain the element of surprise in a war zone dense with enemy movement. And she'd get another chance at doing something big in the Battle of Guadalcanal.

Charlie smiled. "I'd love another crack at a cruiser, sir."

By this point, he trusted Captain Kane's instincts completely. He'd follow him anywhere, particularly if their course promised action against the Japanese. Frankie had brought twelve torpedoes. Still had eight with which she could sink ships.

"Perhaps you will," Kane said. "Let's just hope we don't fall into a trap as neat as the one I laid for you. Our strategy will be bold but our tactics cautious. We can't just be aggressive; we must also be decisive. It's your move, Harrison."

"I believe I'll cede the game, Captain. Well played."

"We'll play again, I hope." He winked. "Maybe a more thoughtful game next time."

Charlie said, "I'd like that, sir."

He didn't tell the captain that he always played fast and aggressive in his first game against an unknown opponent. It was a simple and direct way of testing an adversary's play. In losing, he'd taken the captain's measure without revealing his own skill level.

The next time they played, he'd show the man exactly how fast a learner he was.

CHAPTER SEVENTEEN
CAT AND MOUSE

Bombed at Cavite and battered at Savo Island, Frankie continued to survive and now headed west by northwest along the St. George Channel, looking for another fight.

Cruising submerged, she passed between the islands of Santa Isabel and New Georgia, where the Seventeenth Army had dug in against the Americans.

"Up scope," Charlie said.

He swung the periscope, scanning the view for targets and threatening planes. He knew Santa Isabel was out there to the east, but he couldn't make landfall. The sun glared hazily through a low overcast that reduced visibility to 10,000 yards.

Frankie and her crew itched for another crack at the Imperial Navy. He took his time, hoping to deliver them a nice juicy target.

A smudge of smoke.

He said, "Helmsman, steer three-three-oh."

Charlie hoped the trail of smoke would lead him to a merchant ship or perhaps even a convoy. He imagined what it would be like if he were the captain, carrying the pressure to produce results while trying to keep his crew alive. Making snap decisions of life and death.

He knew he wanted it. Wanted it bad, though he knew he wasn't ready for the burden.

He smiled as the ship's masts came into view. A small merchant, traveling alone. Making way slowly, about six knots. Bearing one-double-oh, range 7,000 yards.

The sea had grown choppy with the change in weather. Frankie showed only a foot of scope. The pulse of the waves limited his visibility.

"Planes, up two feet," he ordered. "All ahead one-third."

His view improved as the scope rose a little higher above the water. The ship's profile came into focus. It smoked heavily, which had led Charlie to it like a trail of breadcrumbs.

He asked the quartermaster for help looking up the ship in the S-55's reference book of Japanese merchant ships.

"I think he's the *Osaka Maru*," the man said. "Twenty-two hundred tons." The Japanese traditionally included the word, *maru*, meaning, "circle," in all their merchant ship names.

"Down scope." He smiled. "Please notify the captain we have a target."

He put the boat on an approach course to intercept the ship's track. The helmsman rang up all ahead full.

Kane arrived bleary-eyed from sleep. "I hope you've got something tasty for me, Harrison. I was having a hell of a dream. Up scope."

Charlie watched the captain as he studied the enemy ship.

"Nice find," Kane said.

"Thank you, sir."

"But he's a Q-ship."

A decoy ship. A wolf in sheep's clothing. A trap.

The captain said, "His draft is shallower than it looks; a torpedo would go straight under him. If we surface to take him out with the deck gun, he'll come at us hard and fast shooting guns he's got hidden under cover. Then he'll zero in on us with sonar after we dive, and rain depth charges on us. It's not worth the risk. We'll give this Jap a wide berth."

The Japanese had converted the merchant into a warship. Some submarine skipper had learned about the use of Q-ships the hard way, and he'd spread the word.

The British had used Q-ships against German U-boats during the Great War. Charlie found it interesting to see the Japanese trying the same tactics. It made him wonder what kind of tricks Frankie could hide up her sleeve to sucker the Japanese or get herself out of a jam.

"Aye, aye, sir," Charlie said. He adjusted course and gave orders to dive to eighty feet.

"Carry on," the captain said. He left to return to his dream.

The S-55 drove up the Slot.

After another twenty minutes, Charlie took another look. He kept up this cycle for the next two hours. In between, he gave orders to maintain trim in the rough waters, ordering water pumped fore and aft as needed. The boat rolled with the pulse of the waves. He took his salt tablets and felt the sweat pour off him. He fidgeted at the routine. The sighting of the Q-ship had given him a taste for action, an itch he couldn't scratch.

Rusty was right about another thing. You had to loosen up to make it in the submarines.

On the next look up top, he almost whooped.

He saw a group of ships tearing down the Slot from the north. At this range, they were barely discernible, but they looked like destroyers. Another raiding party, and a big one. Bearing three-three-oh, range 10,000 yards.

"Left full rudder," Charlie said. "All ahead full." He said to the quartermaster, "Jakes, please inform the captain we have another target."

"Aye, aye, sir."

To the helmsman: "Steer to oh-nine-five."

Then he took another look. The ships were closer now, and he could make out some detail.

The captain returned to the control room, rubbing sleep from his eyes. "Are you the boy who cried, 'Wolf,' Harrison?"

"I've located another Tokyo Express run and put us on an intercept course."

Kane looked through the scope and whistled. "Now we're talking."

Charlie said, "I made out six destroyers, a seaplane carrier, and a seaplane tender. Three of the destroyers are *Asashio* class. Speed, twenty-eight knots. I'm certain the carrier is the *Chitose*."

Sinking the *Chitose* would be a major Allied victory.

The captain ran his hand over his bristling chin. "It'll be a close thing to catch them." Then he nodded. He had to try. "Come right to one-one-oh. Dive. Seventy feet. All ahead flank."

Frankie accelerated to ten knots, a pace she could hold for a half-hour before the exertion drained the battery.

"Battle stations, torpedo attack," Kane said.

The general alarm honked through the boat, electrifying the crew. They rushed to stations.

Reynolds and Rusty arrived to take their posts, Reynolds as assistant approach officer, Rusty as assistant diving officer. The captain filled them in. As plotting officer, Charlie continued to plot the targets on regular sound bearings.

The Japanese weren't zigzagging. Something had put a bee in their bonnet. Frankie's own course headed toward them in a straight line.

She wasn't going to make it in time.

He drew another point on the graph paper. "They're crossing our bow, Captain."

The captain frowned at the plot. The warships were still out of range.

"Planes, forty-five feet," he said.

The boat angled up and leveled off at periscope depth.

"Up scope."

The captain peered into the eyepiece. "Too far away to even chance a long-range, up-the-stern shot. They're going over the hill."

Charlie put his pencil down and sighed.

"Sound contact," Johnson called from the radio room, Marsh being off duty. "To the northwest. Multiple sets of heavy screws. About 6,000 yards."

Kane swiveled the scope for a sweep and froze. "I've got eyes on the targets. Heavy cruisers! Three of 'em, including our old friend, *Furutaka*."

Charlie grinned at the news. Maybe they'd get another shot at the big ship.

"Bearing, one-seven-five," Johnson said.

"They're too far away, and the battery's almost out of juice," the captain said with disgust. He slammed the scope's handles back into place in cold fury. "We're done for now. Secure from battle stations."

Charlie's face burned with frustration. The S-55 had just come from the area the cruisers were passing through. If these ships had shown up before the destroyers, Frankie could have been conned into a good firing position with time to spare.

"It's a cat-and-mouse game," Rusty said. "But the mice run about ten times faster than this old cat." He leaned against the bulkhead, seemingly exhausted by the mere effort of standing.

Reynolds glared at the captain as if the lack of action weren't the boat's fault, nor even that of the fortunes of war, but solely Kane's. "Let me know if we're going to kill any Japs," he growled. "Otherwise, I'll be off duty."

Kane regarded him icily. "You're dismissed, Reynolds."

The boat's harsh environment, the stress, and the lack of a sinking were pushing them all to the edge. Now the officers were starting to get on each other's nerves.

"I'll keep an eye on the cruisers, Captain," Charlie said.

"If their course changes and I see an opportunity, I'll let you know."

"You do that, Harrison. Carry on." Kane left the room.

The boat's roll grew heavy as she entered rougher seas, up to thirty degrees on each side. The humidity in the boat, already torturous, became insufferable. The periscope fogged again.

Water condensed and streamed in tiny rivulets down the bulkheads. The water produced grounds. The grounds started a series of small electrical fires that had to be secured. The fires produced a chain of equipment breakdowns across the boat.

Charlie didn't know who was more likely to do them in, the Japanese or Frankie herself.

CHAPTER EIGHTEEN
PASSING STORM

After the cruisers raced past at a range of 5,000 yards off the port beam, the captain returned to the control room and gave the order to surface. Frankie had missed her shot, but she still had a job to do. Namely, send a flash radio message to Perth about the Japanese armada headed toward Guadalcanal.

Dressed in sou'wester hats and oilskins, Charlie and his lookouts assembled in the access trunk that led up to the main hatch. Kane had told him it was raining on the surface, which explained the steady climb in humidity inside the boat. The S-55 blew clear of the water.

The hatch opened and released the boat's air pressure in a whistling blast. A wave struck the boat. The torrent of cold seawater poured down the hatch.

"Lookouts to the bridge," Charlie gasped.

Northerly winds, gusting at twenty-five knots, moaned across the open sea. The boat rolled heavily on big waves. The ocean, when roused, released colossal forces that reminded the submariners who was really boss here.

Rain drummed on the deck. Thunder growled like a

distant bombing run.

"Refreshing," Billy Ford said and whooped at the gale.

"Eyes peeled, Billy," Charlie said.

The storm had reduced visibility dramatically. The heavy rains had likely grounded the Japanese pilots for the rest of the day, but some planes might still have been patrolling. Mostly, he kept his eyes on the water, watching for an enemy submarine.

"Bridge, stay clear of the antenna," the control room ordered. "We're transmitting."

"Roger," Charlie shouted back.

Another wave washed over the bridge, leaving them all soaked and sputtering.

Something else to tell Evie in his next letter. He'd been writing to her steadily since his near-swim in the Coral Sea, documenting the challenges, tedium, and periodic hilarity aboard the submarine. He kept everything focused on his personal impressions outside of combat to avoid upsetting Evie as well as the military censors enforcing the secrecy rules of the Silent Service.

Rather than distract him, thinking about her as much as he did was getting him through this. He missed her. The little things, in particular. Her smile. Her laugh. The way she touched his arm when he made her laugh. The way she punched it when he teased her. Her scent. Her kiss. The way she looked at him.

When he returned to Brisbane, he'd mail the letters. Maybe he'd even discover a letter from her. He smiled at the possibility. He wondered what she was doing right now.

What she was thinking about. If she still thought of him.

Another wave swamped the bridge. The S-55 bounced on the swells.

Sometimes, he heard Evie calling him in the drone of the machines as he approached the edge of sleep.

Rusty emerged from the hatch. "Permission to relieve you and your men, Charles."

"Granted, Mr. Grady. No activity up here on watch. How goes it with the repairs?"

"Frankie's having a bad day. We cleared the grounds out of the battery, but a valve broke in the starboard engine. There's oil everywhere. We're back on battery power until we get it fixed."

"Mechanics first," Charlie said. "You weren't kidding about that."

"If Pharaoh ran this boat, he would have let the Hebrews go after his first war patrol."

Charlie followed his exhausted men down the ladder and went to sack out. Fresh air had cooled the boat and put the heavy odors in the background where they belonged. He used straps to tie himself down so he wouldn't fall out of bed due to the boat's heavy roll. Otherwise, he didn't mind it. Seasickness had never bothered him.

Lying in his rack, he sensed the boat's trim getting heavier. The captain reduced speed to two-thirds. The bilge pumps worked nonstop to eject water flowing into the boat through the open main air induction. A change in the atmosphere told him the captain closed it.

He'd reached a point where he could feel the boat's status

and condition with his eyes closed. Frankie had gotten into his mind. Rocked like a baby by the waves, he fell into a deep, peaceful sleep understanding he was a part of the boat now, and the boat a part of him. He didn't know how he'd ever be able to sleep again without hearing the constant drone of machinery.

Hours later, he awoke to shouting. He jumped out of his bunk and started for the control room, hands on the bulkheads to steady himself against the roll. The men were cheering.

"What's the word?" he asked Chief Dobbs.

"The Japs got a licking at Guadalcanal. We really socked it to 'em!"

The battle group that had passed the S-55 yesterday had been surprised by an American fleet of four cruisers and five destroyers off Savo Island. These ships sank the *Furutaka* and one destroyer and heavily damaged a second cruiser. During the exchange of deadly salvoes, the Japanese sank a destroyer and damaged two other ships.

Charlie smiled as he absorbed the details. It was a tactical victory; the battle for ultimate possession of Guadalcanal was far from decided, and the IJN still controlled the seas around it at night. It was a major win, however, for the simple fact that Japan, with its limited resources, couldn't afford such losses, while America put new ships to sea every month.

Rusty could have been right that they were in for a long war, but after victories at the Coral Sea, Midway, and Savo Island, winning it seemed inevitable.

The captain smiled at his cheering men, though it was a sour one. No doubt he regretted moving the S-55 off station and into the Slot. He'd missed the battle and the laurels he might have earned. Nearly two weeks into his patrol, and he had nothing to show for it. Every day that passed, pressure mounted to sink a ship or go back to Brisbane empty-handed.

If that happened, the admirals wouldn't blame the faulty torpedo, the vintage boat, or bad luck. They'd blame the captain. If Kane couldn't deliver, they'd find a man who could.

Charlie knew that was unfair, though he also knew that's how the game was played, and he couldn't change it. For his part, he had to hand it to the captain. Kane was doing the best he could with what he had. Charlie couldn't see how he could do any better.

"It's a good thing we were here, sir," he told the captain. "We warned the fleet."

As far as he was concerned, Frankie had played a critical part in the battle.

"Maybe you're right," Kane said.

"Sometimes, there's a good move, but there might be one that's even better."

The captain smiled again. "Fast learner, Harrison."

The next day, the seas calmed, and the tropical sun blazed in a clear sky. While on periscope watch, Rusty discovered the remnants of the Japanese armada steaming back to Rabaul. Geysers boomed out of the sea as General MacArthur's bombers set up a run over them, dropping their payloads from a dizzying altitude of 18,000 feet. An impressive thing to see, though they didn't score a single hit on the compact, fast-moving, zigzagging destroyers.

The captain ordered flank speed to intercept but never got closer than 3,000 yards.

His occasional pronounced blink had grown more frequent, an internal Morse code.

Gritting his teeth with frustration, he called a meeting of his officers.

CHAPTER NINETEEN
THE LION'S DEN

The officers fell into chairs in the wardroom. Grimy and sweaty, hair matted, eyes lined with fatigue, scratching at their beards, they struck Charlie as warlords of some future apocalyptic generation, cavemen living among machines.

"We have two choices," the captain said. He laid out a map of the Solomons.

Reynolds produced a battered pack of cigarettes from his Australian Army surplus shorts and lit one. He exhaled a cloud of smoke.

Kane tapped the St. George Channel with his finger. "Option one is we finish our patrol in the Slot. We still have over a week before we have to start back to Brisbane. If we get a shot, we take it. If we don't, we send a message to Perth so the fleet can handle it."

Reynolds grimaced. "What's option two?"

The captain's finger slid across the map and stopped. "We go to Rabaul."

The men perked up at that. Three hundred miles northwest of Guadalcanal, Rabaul was the most important Japanese base in the South Pacific. It was the hub for the biggest concentration of warships in the Imperial Navy, all tasked with kicking the Americans out of the Solomons.

Minefields and more than forty massive coastal guns defended the harbor. Behind them, 100,000 crack troops. Airfields launching fighters around the clock.

Rusty said, "What does that mean, exactly, sir?"

"It means we skirt around Bougainville and get up here in the area of Duke of York Island. There'll be plenty of traffic running through that area between Rabaul and the entire island chain. If we run into trouble, we can hide around these little islands around Duke of York."

"Our charts aren't exactly reliable, Captain," Rusty reminded him.

The only documentation the Navy had of the area was old Dutch charts from the late nineteenth century. The S-55 risked running aground on shoals, which would chew up the boat and leave them stranded without hope of rescue by friendly forces.

Charlie whistled at the captain's nerve. Submarines often ventured deep into enemy territory, but Rabaul was the lion's den.

Reynolds expelled a stream of smoke. "Do you want to kill Japs, Captain?"

Kane frowned. He'd clearly had it with his exec sounding off. "No, Reynolds. I'm taking us there to switch sides."

"I'll take that as a yes. How bad do you want to kill Japs?"

"Not bad enough to see the men under my command die by doing something stupid."

The exec sucked on his Lucky Strike and put his own

finger on the map. Simpson Harbor.

Rusty paled. "Jesus Christ."

Reynolds was proposing they take the S-55 right to the mouth of the harbor at Rabaul, where they'd stand face to face with the lion.

He said, "If you want to sink Jap ships, this is where they are."

"We'd never get out of there alive," Kane said.

The captain blinked aggressively as he wrestled with the idea. He was *considering* it.

Charlie knew as well as the captain that this might be Frankie's last patrol. With her constant equipment breakdowns, it was all too likely she'd be taken off the line soon and overhauled as the new fleet boats started showing up in the Pacific in greater numbers.

After that, she'd be assigned to Submarine School to help train the next crop of young submarine captains. Men who'd marvel and laugh at her, just the way Charlie had been amazed at the cramped and primitive conditions aboard the R-boat he'd trained on.

And the captain would be captain no more. If he didn't produce results on this patrol, he was finished, and he knew it.

Reynolds said, "If you want to kill Japs, that's where you'll do it. We're talking big ships. Troop transports filled with riflemen. Oil tankers. Freighters packed mast to keel with tanks and ammunition. Maybe even a cruiser or a flattop. They all sail through Rabaul." He stabbed his cigarette into the ashtray. "But again, it depends on how bad you want to kill them."

Charlie marveled at the man's ferocity. Before he considered his choice of words or whether he should say them at all, he asked, "Why do you hate them so much?"

"Because," Reynolds said, "none of your fucking business, Lieutenant."

"Harrison is right," Kane said. "If I even consider your option, I want to know what you're thinking. If this is just some score you're looking to settle with the Japs—"

"I do have a score to settle with the Japs. One in particular. I'm looking for a destroyer. It may be at Rabaul. It may not. But odds are, I'll run into him again eventually."

The men waited, but he said nothing more. He produced another cigarette and lit it.

Everybody hated the Japanese. They were an alien race, but that had nothing to do with why Americans hated them. Americans hated them for the simple fact the Japanese Navy had bombed Pearl Harbor. If Brazil had bombed Pearl, Americans would hate Brazilians. It was simple, really. But Reynolds's hatred bordered on pathological.

Charlie believed the exec had a vendetta against the captain of the destroyer that had sunk the S-56 in the Banda Sea. He thought of the screams that flooded out of the stateroom where the exec bunked. He wondered what the man saw in his dreams that could produce such terror.

Kane said, "Suppose Frankie makes it that far without everything going broke dick. Suppose we find a sweet spot in the bay. Suppose we don't trigger God-knows-what sonar alarms they've got rigged up. Suppose patrolling destroyers don't zero in on us and give us the beating of our lives."

Reynolds said, "That's entirely—"

"Suppose we see a convoy and release every fish in our tubes. Suppose the setup and the equipment all works just beautifully, and we sink four ships, including your destroyer. Suppose all that. How do we get the hell out? They'll be all over us in a flash and box us in."

Reynolds had no answer to that.

Charlie thought of the Q-ship. An idea came to him in a flash. "We decoy them, sir."

Kane leaned on the table. So did Reynolds. Charlie explained his idea, which was simple enough. The veteran officers immediately improved upon it and made it practical.

Rusty laughed nervously. "We're not really thinking about doing this, are we?"

The captain scratched at his beard. "I don't know. Maybe. I mean, it's still a hell of a risk. The whole thing's a crapshoot."

The men quietly considered the massive rewards as well as the astounding risk.

"I won't ask you again if you want to kill Japs," Reynolds said. "I know you do. Every red-blooded American sailor does. But I'll ask again: How bad do you want to kill Japs?"

Charlie still struggled with the question. Was he willing to die?

If it ended the war, he thought he was. But sinking a few important ships, while possibly altering the strategic balance in the Solomons, might have little major impact on the overall war. Even if it shortened it by as much as a month, was that worth dying for?

Hell, that was assuming they sank any ships at all. That was assuming the IJN didn't detect them, pin them down with destroyers, and send them to the bottom forever before they shot off a single torpedo.

Answering Reynolds's question meant quantifying the conditions under which he would be willing to die for a cause. Charlie just couldn't do that. But a primitive urge propelled him to take the risk. Blame it on foolish youth's innate sense of immortality—the young man's war cry, "It can't happen to me!" Blame it on the same crazy desire that drove the first men up Mount Everest.

In the end, Charlie wanted to do it to see if he could and live to tell the tale.

Kane said, "I know where the exec stands on this. Rusty, what do you think?"

"I think it's too much risk." He snarled at Reynolds, "Talk about a knife to a gunfight."

"Harrison?"

"We have a way in and a way out," Charlie started but then stopped. He cut to the bottom line. "The whole thing is obviously a big risk, but so is going to Duke of York Island. Going straight to Rabaul is just one more level of risk but with rewards that are much bigger."

The reasoning appealed to the analytical Kane.

"I'm inclined to agree," he said. "Here's what we're going to do. We'll go north. If we shoot our wad before we get there and sink some ships along the way, we turn back. If not, we go to the harbor and take a look around, feel out the defenses. If Frankie's up for it and we can get a good shot at some ships, by God, we'll take it. If not, we'll beat it for somewhere safer. Agreed?"

There were a lot of "ifs" there, but the captain had laid out a logical flow of decisionmaking. It all seemed sensible to Charlie.

"Roger," Reynolds said.

"Aye, aye, sir," Charlie said.

"Hoo-ray," Rusty said at his sarcastic best.

"All right then. Reynolds, conn the boat into a course for Rabaul. Dismissed."

In the passageway, Rusty said to Charlie, "Now Evie's really going to be furious with you."

"I'm sorry, Rusty. I had to speak my mind. I honestly think we can do it."

The engineering officer stared at him as if to say, *What the hell do you really know about it?* He said, "You think we can do it because you want to do it. Simple as that. This isn't an adventure film starring Douglas Fairbanks. This is real, with real consequences. In real life, the good guy, the hero, he dies all the time."

Charlie didn't know what to say to that. Rusty was right, but he was wrong. Damn it, this was war. War was full of risks. Somebody had to take a big risk, or they'd never win.

"Listen, the captain's made up his mind in any case," he said. "He's got a good plan. Don't get so worked up about it. Hell, we might end up not even doing it in the end if the risks are too bad. Captain Kane has good judgment. I trust him."

Rusty shook his head sadly. "A captain trying to save his career, an exec who's got a personal vendetta against some Jap Moby Dick, and a young lieutenant who just knows it's all going to be fine. Sure, I'll trust you guys. I'll trust you with my life."

Charlie recoiled, stung. "Jesus, Rusty."

"Wishing the Japs dead isn't going to make them dead. Like I said, this is real. Think about what Evie's going to be feeling when she gets a letter from the Navy saying you're missing and presumed lost. Think about what my Lucy's going to feel. My son, who'll grow up without his daddy. Because we're going to die up there, Charlie. We're going to die."

CHAPTER TWENTY
ONE MAN TO TELL THE TALE

Billy Ford shook him awake. "The exec needs you topside, Mr. Harrison."

Charlie rolled over. "Beat it, Billy."

"He said he needed you." Another shake. "Sir?"

"Did Braddock tell you to get me?"

"No. Mr. Reynolds did."

Charlie bolted out of his bunk and put on his sandals. "Thanks, Billy."

He climbed the ladder up the main access trunk but didn't find Reynolds on the bridge.

One of the lookouts pointed. "He's down there, sir."

Charlie found the executive officer standing on the main deck. The storm had passed, and the boat floated on moderate seas rolling with white caps. The bow broke the waves and flung spray. The air tasted like brine. The sky was black and full of stars.

"You asked to see me?"

After the disastrous attack on the *Furutaka* at Savo Island, Reynolds had stopped coming down on him. He obviously believed that, from then on, the war had much more to teach

Charlie.

This wasn't about instruction. The executive officer wanted a private conversation with him.

"We just got a radio message," the exec said. "Two Jap battleships shelled Henderson Field. They came close to destroying it. They're going to try another offensive soon to retake the island."

Charlie shook his head at the news. Though victory often appeared rationally inevitable, it just as often felt impossible. As Rusty had warned him, the Japanese were good at war, and they never gave up. Since August, thousands of Americans had died in a war of attrition just to maintain their toehold in the Solomons. At this rate, it might take a decade and only God knew how many lives before they reached the Japanese home islands.

Reynolds said, "You asked me why I hate the Japs so much."

"You were right. It's none of my business."

"I'm not sure that kind of thinking applies anymore on this boat, Harrison. It's possible we won't be coming back."

Reynolds wanted to unburden himself of his nightmare, and he'd chosen Charlie as his confessor. Charlie no longer felt sure he wanted to hear his confession. He was already scared.

He said, "Do you think we'll get out of Rabaul alive?"

The exec considered his answer. "We can blame this broke-dick boat all we want, but at some point, we have to take a chance. If we don't get in the war, we're just taking up space."

Charlie had to agree with that.

Then Reynolds told his story, and Charlie listened to every word.

The S-56 had fought a running battle during the retreat from the Philippines. In the Banda Sea, the captain stopped the boat for repairs near Gunung Api, a small island west of Papua New Guinea. That night, a patrolling Japanese destroyer found them.

The *Mizukaze*, Japanese for "water wind."

"A *Minekaze*-class DD, 1,600 tons," Reynolds elaborated. "An old ship, not nearly as good as the newer Fubuki- and *Asashio*-class DDs. The Japs use their older DDs for merchant escort and coastal defense. The ship had no business being way out there, but there he was, and he came steaming at us with a bone in his teeth at forty knots."

The S-56 dived and rigged for silent running as the destroyer thrashed overhead. The ship dropped a pattern of depth charges.

"I remember seeing Captain Scully smile as the explosions rattled the boat. He always did that during a depth charging. He'd break out in a grin like we were kids who'd pulled an epic prank. Then we'd all smile. We knew we were going to be all right."

The S-56 shook off her pursuer and surfaced, but the destroyer came at her again.

"That Jap skipper was a bloodhound. He kept at us day and night. No matter what we did, he always knew where we were and stayed on top of us. By the third day, we were in trouble. The battery was almost flat. We were out of air.

We were going to have to go up and fight it out. Our tubes were dry. All we had was the four-inch deck gun and machine guns."

They fought in darkness. Tracer rounds flashed between the two vessels. The S-56 scored a hit on the bridge, which disoriented the destroyer, but the ship's 120-mm guns kept the fire hot. Hills of water rose up around the boat. After a long running battle, a salvo struck her engine room, ejecting flaming debris and bodies across the water.

The S-56 stopped dead. Another shell punched a hole in her motor room below the water line. Smoke billowed from the engine room. Water sprayed high above the stern. The boat groaned and shifted as water gushed inside, drowning the men in the sealed aft compartments.

"The captain tried to surrender. Men jumped up and down on the deck shouting their heads off and waving sheets. The destroyer kept firing. Another salvo blew the deck gun clear into the water. Scully gave orders to abandon ship. Twelve hands made it off the boat before she sank like a stone. The captain said to me, 'It's me they want. God be with you.' He knew what they'd do to him to get information. He went down with the boat."

The sailors found themselves in a seething sea that was alive with snakes.

"They were everywhere. Thousands. The locals call them cigarette snakes."

Wide-eyed, Charlie asked, "Are they poisonous?"

"They're called cigarette snakes because, after you get bit, you have time to enjoy one last smoke before you die."

The sailors screamed and thrashed at the snakes. Two men were bitten. Wearing life jackets, they stayed afloat, their dead faces bobbing in the water. The rest fought to stay calm as the snakes, normally not aggressive, writhed curiously around their warm bodies.

"The destroyer steamed past nice and slow. The Japs lined the gunwales in their clean white uniforms and pointed down at us. Many appeared sickened by the sight of us wrapped in an endless floating carpet of snakes. Others laughed. An officer had a rifle and did some target practice shooting at our heads. That's when I saw the Jap skipper. He was short and had a flat face that looked down at us without any expression. Like his face was carved of wood. Like we weren't human beings he was looking at, but ants that were being stepped on. The officer took a shot at me. Moore's skull popped like a grape in the corner of my eye. Something warm struck my ear. While the Japs cheered, I thought, 'I've never truly known hate until now.'"

The destroyer left them to die in the sea. The sailors clung to each other, floating on the cold current while hundreds of snakes crawled over them. One man fell into shock and went under, never to emerge. Another simply gave up and let himself die.

The next day, the scorching tropical sun beat down on seven survivors. Unrelenting heat and thirst. Their only relief was that they floated away from the snakes. That night, the sharks came.

"Big hammerheads. I know they were hammerheads because I saw one rear out of the water and rip one of the manifoldmen in half with a single bite."

The survivors shouted to each other in the dark, trying to maintain contact. One by one, the men screamed and sank out of sight. The next morning, only Reynolds and Heller, the soundman, remained alive.

They started jury rigging a raft from some debris floating on the water.

"We drifted along while it got dark again. I saw some drifting planks of wood and swam off to get them. When I looked back, Heller was gone. I called out to him and got no answer. I was alone. After another day of that unending hell, I knew I was going to die. Drifting in the dark, I saw my wife and children, my mom and dad. I voiced all my regrets and gratitude and said goodbye to them. I grew up in Kansas all over again, saw the odd turns of life that led me to the Naval Academy and a life on the boats. I saw flashes in the dark as the destroyer punched holes in the 56 and blew her guts into the sea. I saw Scully say, 'God be with you,' as he disappeared down the hatch to die with his boat. I heard the terrified screams of the men—men I'd served with, men I loved and called my friends—as they died in the water."

The moon emerged from the clouds, and he saw the dead faces of the entire crew bobbing in the water. For the rest of the night, he heard them screaming.

Some locals rowed out in a sampan and pulled him out of the water raving. They handed him over to some Dutch missionaries passing by on a refugee ship. An American patrol boat stopped the ship near the Australian coastal city of Cairns and took Reynolds aboard.

At a hospital in Cairns, he healed his ravaged body and faked his way through repeated psychiatric evaluations. He returned to duty and reported as exec to the S-55. He would have taken any job the Navy offered him, as long as he got to kill Japs, but he particularly enjoyed being executive officer. As exec on a sugar boat, he got to push the firing button.

"I'd like to stand here and say my faith in God pulled me through, my love for my family, an indestructible will to live, but that part of me died in the Banda Sea when I said goodbye to everything I ever loved. The only thing that got me through was my hate for that Jap ship and its heartless skipper who looked down at us like we weren't even there."

The exec turned to wipe tears from his face. Of rage or loss, Charlie didn't know. He looked away, stunned by what he'd heard.

Reynolds said, "Now you know how bad I want to kill Japs, Harrison. And that I'm going to sink the *Mizukaze* no matter how long it takes, no matter what the cost."

CHAPTER
TWENTY-ONE
RABAUL

Fortress Rabaul. The lion's den. A hub of merchant shipping that was the lifeblood of an empire that controlled one-tenth of the world. Home of the IJN's Eighth Fleet.

Located on the northeastern tip of New Britain, the town had been built in a sunken caldera along the natural anchorage of Simpson Harbor. Forested mountains loomed beyond the town. Vulcan Volcano smoked in the western jungle.

Before the Japanese came, the island had been an Australian territory. Australian units had been sent to fight in North Africa, leaving the garrison depleted. The Japanese landed in January 1942, swept aside the defenders, and hunted them down in the jungle. Then they turned the town into an impregnable land, air, and naval base ringed by artillery and anti-aircraft guns.

The captain studied the harbor defenses through the periscope and whistled at the view. His officers eyed him anxiously.

"All ahead one-third," he said. "Steady as she goes."

The S-55 crept as close to the harbor mouth as Kane dared take her.

"I see a lot of ships tied up," he observed. "What do you think, Reynolds? They're all lined up in a row, like sitting ducks. Maybe we should go in there and take them out."

"I was thinking, we could skirt around—"

"I was joking, Reynolds."

Entering the harbor would be suicide. Assuming the S-55 could navigate the minefields without being blown out of the water, she'd have to stay out of contact of roaming patrol boats. Then she'd be in shallow waters—clearly visible and with nowhere to dive deep to escape.

They'd just have to wait until some ships came out.

The problem was they only had enough fuel and provisions for four days before they had to turn back for Brisbane. They had no idea when a ship might emerge from the harbor mouth. It might be hours, it might be days, maybe even weeks.

"It's too bad," Kane said. "I can see the meatballs on their sides." Japanese naval insignia, a blood-red sun on a white field. "Makes a nice target."

Sound waves thudded against the hull. Distant booms.

The men glanced at each other.

"MacArthur's bombers," the captain said. "It's raining hell up there. The B-17s are stirring up the hornets' nest. I see Zeros flying everywhere. Down scope. Helm, right full rudder."

"Right full rudder, aye, Captain," answered the

helmsman. He turned the wheel.

"I wonder how they like having bombs dropped on their heads," Rusty said.

"Come to east," Kane ordered. "Maintain speed. All compartments, stand by to dive."

He was turning the boat around. The S-55 was visible from the air, and although the Zeros were preoccupied with the bombers overhead, Kane was wisely avoiding any risk of detection. He didn't want the enemy to know he was there until his first torpedo hit.

More than that, he wanted to get as far away from the bombing as possible. The B-17 "flying fortresses" weren't precision weapons; they dropped big sledgehammers from 18,000 feet. It would be in keeping with Frankie's luck to have come all this way to the lion's den only to be sunk by an errant 500-pound bomb made in the U.S.A.

"Dive. Eighty feet. Battery, how much juice do we have in the can?"

The hull vibrated with booms thudding in rapid succession.

The telephone talker relayed the battery room's answer. The captain nodded, satisfied.

"All ahead flank."

The submarine glided across Blanche Bay to safer waters.

The captain clapped Charlie on the shoulder. "Wait and hurry up, Harrison."

"Yes, sir," Charlie said with a smile.

He felt the same excitement that infected the rest of the crew, who imagined returning to base with a broom tied to the shears and several meatballs painted on the hull.

The broom signified a "clean sweep," a patrol in which all torpedoes were fired. The meatball insignia were brags of ships sunk.

He didn't think they'd have to wait much longer. The bombing was likely to get the Japanese thinking about accelerating departure schedules. Ships might be on the move soon.

The S-55 would reach Duke of York Island by nightfall. There, her engines would recharge the battery. Then the old sea wolf would become a hunter. And return to Simpson Harbor.

"Why don't you get some rest?" Kane suggested.

When the captain made a suggestion, it was best to consider it an order. "Aye, aye, sir."

"You too, Rusty. Don't worry, you won't miss anything."

The officers retired to their stateroom and collapsed on their bunks. Charlie stared at the bulkhead, thinking of everything and nothing at the same time, his mind racing but unable to fix on a specific point. Rusty appeared to be in the same condition. He picked up his thick book and tried to read, but he put it away. Then he started a letter but crumpled up the page minutes later.

"It's funny how you bring a book on a patrol, and you don't think it might be the last book you ever read," he said. "You write a letter to home, and you never think, 'This is it. This is the last thing I'll ever say to them.' But when you do think it, it becomes impossible to read or write. Then it becomes impossible to think at all. All you know is you don't want to die."

Charlie said, "I understand."

"There's so much to read, so much to say. So many things to do in life, and if we die, we won't get to do a single one of them. We'll be gone."

Charlie thought about Reynolds saying goodbye to his family and coming to terms with his death. Even after his rescue, he never stopped believing he was dead.

The Japanese had a warrior philosophy about that. *Bushido*, it was called. To be a warrior who fights without fear, he must already accept that he's dead.

Reynolds was fearless, and he'd paid the price to get that way. Charlie wasn't fearless, he was, well, foolhardy. The closer he got to the moment of truth, the more he realized that fact.

"Try not to think about it, Rusty," he said. "Otherwise, you'll drive yourself crazy."

"But what if I do die and I never say what I need to say to Lucy and my son? All right. I'm doing it." He reopened his journal and began to scribble. "I'm writing, 'I love you. I'm sorry. Be happy.'" Then he tore the page out of the notebook and handed it to Charlie. "If I don't make it back, you'll give that to Lucy. You'll tell her about me."

"I will, Rusty. But I won't need to send it."

"And don't sugar coat it. I want you to tell her I was crapping my pants. No hero shit. I want you to tell her I was thinking of her and Russell Junior at the very end. Tell her the truth."

Charlie folded the paper and put it in his pocket. "I'm just glad that your dying thought won't be, 'Charlie got me into this mess.'"

Rusty laughed. "If I'm about to die, the last person I'll be thinking about is you, no offense." He grew pensive again. "You know, I think you have a death wish. I'm not picking on you. I'm picking on every stupid young lieutenant in this Navy. The sad thing is you don't even know you have it. And the only way you'll learn you actually do is by dying. If we get out of this with laurels, you'll go on calling it something else, and it'll only get worse."

"I don't want to die. I'm scared too. But I want to win. I want to do my part. Life isn't enough. I want to do something important."

He didn't want to be like Reynolds. As much as he admired the man's strength, he didn't think the exec could ever go home. Whether alive or dead, Reynolds wouldn't survive the war.

"The war doesn't matter," Rusty said. "Only life does. I hope you survive it, Charlie. Get married and produce another life. Then you'll know what I'm talking about."

"If I'd known you were going to be such an over-thinking, morbid son of a bitch, I would have roomed with the exec. All he does is scream all night."

Rusty smiled. He took a deep breath. "Whatever happens, happens. Right?"

"We're going to be okay."

"You keep saying that. You know ... Well, just in case, it's been an honor and all that."

They shook hands warmly.

"Same here," Charlie told him. "I don't think I would have gotten along with Frankie half as much if you hadn't been here. I'm proud to call you my friend, Rusty. Would you do me one more big favor?"

"Sure. That's what friends are for."

Charlie took out his journal and wrote, *My dearest Evie, I love you. I'm sorry. Be happy.* He read the words aloud and meant them as he said them. Then he tore out the page and handed it over. "If anything happens to me, I want you give this to my Evelyn."

"I'll send it," Rusty said. "And if you survive this patrol, maybe I'll send it anyway and do you the biggest favor of your life."

CHAPTER TWENTY-TWO

THE FINAL GAME

The long night brought no action. Ships came and went, mostly destroyers. When a freighter emerged from the harbor with a naval auxiliary escort, Charlie felt sure the S-55 would attack. Kane conned the boat into a firing position but never declared battle stations. The captain, performing his calculations of risk and profit, saw a good move but decided to wait for a better one. By the time the boat returned to Duke of York, Charlie felt anxious enough to chew through the bulkhead.

After two hours of deck watch, he cleared the bridge and headed back below deck. The boat's battery recharged. At 2200, she dived and began her slow return to Simpson Harbor, gliding across Blanche Bay at a depth of eighty feet.

Charlie was off duty but felt too excited to sleep. He plodded into the wardroom with a cup of coffee and began dealing a game of solitaire.

The captain entered with his pipe and sat. "We'll attack soon, Harrison."

"Wait and hurry up," Charlie said.

"Would you have taken a shot at the freighter?"

He thought about it. "A bird in the hand is worth two in the bush, sir."

The captain nodded but didn't explain his decision. Charlie guessed personal reasons were taking a strong role in the man's decisionmaking. The captain had come to Rabaul. He wasn't going home without a big win.

"We have time," the captain said. "In fact, we even have time for another chess game."

Charlie put away the cards. Kane let him play as white.

"Which is fitting," the man explained. "A submariner always starts with the initiative. Let's see if you know how to hold it while I depth charge your offense."

"Battle stations," Charlie muttered. He set up the pieces while the captain lit his pipe.

"After a while, you start to develop a strong sense of intuition around this business," Kane said. "I've got a good feeling about our position here. I think we're going to score big."

"I hope you're right," Charlie said. He still trusted the captain's instincts and admired the man personally. He certainly hoped Kane was right about what his gut was telling him. He'd served on the S-55 for several weeks now and suffered equipment malfunctions, oppressive conditions, and a horrific depth charging, but he still hadn't seen a single Jap ship sink.

"I've gotten to develop a pretty good instinct about men as well," Kane added. "Whippersnappers like you, Harrison. I think you'll go far in the submarines."

"Thank you, sir." Charlie waited, hoping to receive detailed feedback on his performance—and craving more praise. But the captain didn't elaborate. "I think I can do some good here."

"It's a young man's business. The conditions, the new doctrines. Men like me, we're on our way out. The Navy's going to need good skippers. Come on, make your move."

Charlie moved a pawn, too flustered to think straight. The captain countered. Then he put aside his swirling ideas and doubts about his competence as a submarine officer and focused on the game. He wanted to impress the captain by giving him the drubbing of his life. He took his time developing his assault, admiring the potential energy coiled within the array of pieces. It struck him how similar the effort was to conning a boat into an ideal firing position.

The captain traded pieces in an attempt to disrupt his opponent's initiative, but Charlie maintained the pressure.

"You've got your eye on the prize this game," the captain said. "Fast learner, indeed."

Charlie moved his queen across the board. "Check."

"In fact, I am starting to believe that you were just sizing me up during our first game."

"That would be deceptive, sir."

The captain guffawed at that. "Next time, I'll know exactly what to—"

A messenger poked his head in the doorway. "Mr. Reynolds requests you on the bridge, Captain. He's made contact with a Jap convoy!"

CHAPTER TWENTY-THREE

BATTLE STATIONS

The captain and Charlie hurried to the control room. Reynolds welcomed them with a rare smile and said, "We've got a sound contact on a convoy."

"The lion's come out of his den," the captain said. "Talk to me, Marsh."

"Six contacts, heavy screws," the soundman answered. "Bearing, one-one-oh. Range, 3,000 yards." He counted screw turns. "Speed, about ten knots."

"Anything that sounds like an escort?"

"Two sets of fast screws, one to the convoy's port and the other astern."

"Very well." To Reynolds: "What's our heading?"

"Holding steady at two-seven-oh."

"Show me."

The executive officer pointed out the convoy positions and the S-55 on the plot. Rusty was plotting based on Marsh's sound bearings.

The captain frowned at the plot, performing mental

calculations. Charlie recognized the look from their chess games. The sweating men at their stations stared at him, waiting.

"Battle stations, torpedo attack," Kane said.

The battle stations alarm honked throughout the boat.

"Battle stations, torpedo," the quartermaster announced over the public address.

All hands rushed to stations. Charlie grinned. This was it.

The captain initiated the attack approach.

"Helm, come left to two-eight-oh," he ordered.

"Come left to two-eight-oh, aye, sir," the helmsman answered.

"All compartments report battle stations manned, Captain," the telephone talker reported.

"Very well." He added in a loud voice, "This one's for all the marbles, boys. So let's do it right. We sink 'em, we get out, and we go home."

The men let out a ragged cheer.

Kane threw Reynolds a meaningful look and tapped the plot. The captain was maneuvering the S-55 ahead of the convoy and onto their starboard side, where he'd set up a good firing position. The merchant ships would pass broadside, presenting large targets at close range. The destroyer escorts would be on the other side of the merchants.

"That's where we'll take them."

"Roger that," the exec said.

"We'll intercept their track using sound bearings. Come up to periscope depth right about here."

"That doesn't leave a lot of time to designate the targets. It's pitch black out there."

"I want minimal chance of detection. We'll raise scope at 1,500 yards. You shoot when I say shoot. I'm hoping to put at least two ships in the bag. Two fish at each."

"Roger."

"Then we dive, show them Harrison's trick, and get the hell out."

The captain turned to watch the plot develop. The targets were moving south through Blanche Bay. The S-55 cruised southwest to swing around and meet them on their starboard side.

"Sometimes, we get lucky," the captain said. "Eh, Rusty?"

Rusty nodded, looking pale. Sweat dripped off his nose and chin onto the plotting paper. He was trembling. The captain put a reassuring hand on his shoulder.

The engineering officer stopped shaking and said, "Yeah. Sometimes, we do."

"Take over as assistant diving officer, Rusty. Harrison will carry on with the plotting."

The captain smiled. He didn't appear to be nervous at all. In fact, he looked downright happier than Charlie had ever seen him. The die had been cast. Whatever happened, happened, and he'd given it his best shot. The man felt free, Charlie realized.

Charlie just hoped his trick worked. He felt certain it would, but that was only his opinion, and one born in his gut and not from experience. In reality, anything could happen, and the boat and the lives of the crew would be in his hands at the crucial moment.

Kane said, "Left full rudder. Come to north."

"Left full rudder, come to north, aye, sir," the helmsman acknowledged.

The S-55 began her sweeping arc under the water. The Japanese convoy plowed steadily toward her. The ships weren't zigzagging. They cruised south, oblivious that the sea's most dangerous predator was hunting them.

"Fathometer reading."

The fathometer measured water depth under the keel. The convoy was protected by land on one flank and a destroyer behind and on the other flank. By putting the S-55 between the ships and the coast, the captain risked running aground in shallow waters.

"One hundred forty feet, Captain."

"Very well. Keep those soundings coming. Helm, left full rudder. Come to east."

Charlie studied the plot. They were on the enemy's track now. Like a chess game, though this was no game.

He had to hand it to the captain. The man knew his business. His patience was paying off.

"Reduce speed to one-third."

"Reduce speed to one-third, aye," came the reply.

"Fathometer reading?"

"Eighty feet, Captain."

"Very well. Bisby, we're going to do this on the fly," the captain told the helmsman. "Once the scope is raised, I'll identify the first target and shout out an adjustment in heading."

"Aye, aye, Captain."

Range to target was now 1,800 yards and closing.

"It's show time. Planes, forty-five feet."

The boat tilted up and leveled off.

"Good trim at forty-five feet," Rusty reported.

"Torpedo room, make ready the tubes. Order of tubes is one, two, three, four. Set the depth at four feet. Zero gyro angle."

In the bow torpedo compartment, men loaded the torpedoes into their firing tubes and slammed the hatches shut. The tubes flooded. The outer doors opened.

"All four tubes ready to fire, Captain," Reynolds said.

The tension in the control room had become palpable.

"Very well. Up scope."

The periscope rose. Kane gripped the handles and frowned. He slammed the handles back into place with a loud clap. "Down scope."

The men glanced at each other. Something was wrong.

"Fogged again," he growled. "I can't see a goddamn thing up there. Luck comes and goes on this boat. All right, we're still doing this. Raise the number one scope."

The S-55 was equipped with two periscopes. The 1.5-inch number two scope, with its smaller profile, was used for attack. The four-inch number one periscope was used for general observation. It was more visible on the surface, but that couldn't be helped.

Charlie's gaze took in the old pipes running along the bulkhead, the droning machines, the rows of bright lights on the boards. He prayed, *Frankie, don't do this. Don't let us down.*

The periscope groaned alarmingly as it rose in short, jerky steps. Then it jammed in train.

"DAMN IT!" Kane raged. The men flinched. He barked out a short spiteful laugh. "I can't believe it. We're *blind*." He added under his breath, "Fuck this fucking boat."

The men stared at him with frustration and despair. The attack was failing. Marsh called out a sound bearing. The ships were closing. Soon, they would cross the submarine's bow. Kane could try to fix the periscopes, but that would take time.

By then, the convoy would be gone, and the slow-moving submarine would have no chance of catching them.

Rusty grabbed a screwdriver and went to work. "It's thoroughly jammed. I need an auxiliaryman."

Another sound bearing.

Reynolds took the screwdriver and elbowed him aside. He wedged the tool into the faulty bearing and jigged it. His movements became more frantic, his sweating face flushed with rage. He shoved the scope, which shook in its mounting.

"That'll do," Kane said.

The exec shoved it again and stepped back panting.

The captain vented his frustration with a sigh. He touched the bulkhead by way of apology to Frankie for swearing at her. "You know, I'm about ready to hang up my hat and let a younger, stupider man do this job." He glared up at the bulkhead and added fiercely, "But not yet."

He scratched at his bearded jaw, doing his calculations. His eyes clenched in a blink.

"Helm, come right forty-five degrees," he said. "All compartments, stand by to surface."

The men frowned at him, unsure whether they'd heard him correctly.

Captain Kane said, "We're going to fight them on the water."

CHAPTER TWENTY-FOUR

SURFACE ATTACK

Rigged for red and ready to surface on Kane's order.

He said, "As soon as the first ship in the starboard column passes, we'll surface and shoot two fish at him. Then we'll swing to port and shoot the next two fish at the second ship as he approaches. After that, we'll dive, and we'll dive fast."

Reynolds asked, "Should we start the engines while we're up there?"

The captain thought about it. "There's going to be a lot of floating metal moving around. We're boxed in against the coast here. We might need to run before we dive. So yes, fire up the diesels, and give me both mains on propulsion."

"Very good, sir," the exec said, satisfied in every respect.

"You'll carry on as assistant approach officer, Rusty as assistant diving officer. I'll be on the bridge and will provide firing control and steering directions from there."

Charlie had listened to the exchange with breathless excitement. A moment of catharsis as he realized they still had a shot at the Japanese ships, however dangerous.

For an S-boat to launch a night surface attack on a defended convoy was unheard of. But it could be done, and it could be successful. They had the element of surprise.

Kane added, "Harrison, you'll be coming to the bridge with me."

"Aye, aye, sir," Charlie said, his heart pounding loud enough to compete with the boat's mechanical hum.

"You'll maintain a watch of two good men plus yourself. I want eyes on all sides. If they see something, they tell you, you tell me. Understand?"

"Roger that, sir." He said to the yeoman, "Call Fredericks and Peters to the control room."

"Aye, aye, sir."

The captain said, "Reynolds, if I'm killed or incapacitated, you will take command and dive the boat. Dive the boat and get the hell out of here. Is that clear? Get these men home."

"Roger, Captain."

A set of heavy screws churned the water. The first ship was close. Whatever type of ship it was, it was big.

"Surface," Kane said.

The surfacing alarm sounded. The manifoldmen blew high-pressure air into the main ballast tanks. The boat rose gently like an elevator with the planes set at a zero angle.

The lookouts hung binoculars around their necks and climbed up the access trunk ladder into the cramped conning tower. The glass ports showed nothing but inky darkness. The view began to swirl with bioluminescent foam as the S-55 broke the surface.

Charlie didn't have time to judge whether the captain's

plan was audacious or suicidal. It would be the final irony that they all died because of a broke-dick periscope.

"Open the hatch," Kane ordered.

The quartermaster cracked the hatch to allow the boat's built-up air pressure to vent into the atmosphere.

The captain regarded Charlie. "This is it, Harrison. Let's get it done."

"Aye, aye, Captain."

"Lookouts to the bridge."

Charlie thought of Evie. *I love you. I'm sorry. Be happy.*

Then he went up the hatch and out into the night.

"Stand by, torpedo room," Kane said once they'd reached the bridge.

"I've got him, sir." Charlie pointed. "There. That's his wake. Eight hundred yards."

He raised his binoculars and scanned the darkness for the next ship in line. He caught a glimmer of the ship's bow wake and called it out.

Right now, Charlie was looking at the starboard column of a Japanese convoy.

The captain grinned. "Amazing. They haven't spotted us. We're sitting pretty, Harrison."

Charlie estimated the angle on the bow to starboard for the first ship and to port for the second ship. The captain corrected his estimates like a patient schoolteacher.

He said into the intercom, "Ready ... Fire one."

"Firing one!" came the reply.

The boat shuddered as a ton of metal rushed out of its tube and streaked toward the empty waters in front of the receding black shape.

Charlie counted eight seconds.

"Fire two," the captain said.

"Firing two!"

"Swing to port," Kane ordered. "Shifting targets. Stand by, torpedo room."

"Swinging to port. Torpedo room, standing by."

"Meet her, meet her. Steady!"

Charlie scanned the dark. No sign of the escorts.

"Ready ... Fire three."

"Firing three!"

After six seconds: "Fire four."

The boat shuddered again as her last torpedo swished from its tube.

Charlie checked their wakes. "Torpedoes running true, Captain."

He turned, ready to clear the bridge, but Kane ordered, "Torpedo, reload tubes one and two. Helm, come right to east."

Charlie counted the seconds. At this range, the first torpedo should have hit by now. He'd lost sight of its wake as it sped off into the distant dark.

From across the water, he heard a man shout something in Japanese. Raising an alarm.

"Captain—"

A colossal boom shook the night. The entire sky flared white. Charlie blinked in the aftermath of the flash and trained his binoculars on the impact.

The ship was on fire. The torpedo had blown its stern off.

Charlie caught sight of its profile and roiling clouds of black smoke. Tiny figures, some of them on fire, jumped into the water.

"Jesus Christ," Charlie said. It was a spectacular sight, both cathartic and sickening.

"Solid hit on the starboard target," Kane told the control room. "Helm, steady on this course." Then he said to his lookouts, "Eyes peeled, gentlemen. We're still in the game."

The next ship in line tooted his whistle to warn the convoy of a submarine attack. The merchant fired wildly into the dark. Within moments, tracer rounds burst from every ship in view. Searchlights frantically swept the water.

The submarine shook. A geyser erupted from the water 500 yards to port. He scanned the view for the destroyer escorts.

"That was a premature," the captain said. The defective torpedo had exploded in the water before it reached its target. Meanwhile, the other torpedo fired at the starboard target appeared to have missed.

The last torpedo streaked toward the second ship.

The ship turned hard to port to evade. The torpedo caught him amidships with a powerful detonation that flung a cloud of debris into the sky.

"Solid hit on the port-side target," Kane grinned.

The torpedo had broken his back, a mortal blow.

Debris splashed into the water. A smoking chunk of metal banged across Frankie's main deck and splashed in the water.

"Reload completed on number one tube," Reynolds

reported from the control room.

"Where are those escorts, Harrison?"

"I can't get eyes on them, sir. They must be caught up in the tangle."

"All ahead full," the captain said.

The boat accelerated on both mains, taking her directly into the gap between the columns. The first ship they'd torpedoed groaned as it began to sink by the stern. The bow of the second was sinking rapidly under a massive fountain of spraying water, dragging the stern down with it.

"Jesus," Charlie breathed. He went back to looking for the escorts.

Another jolt. A flash of light to starboard.

"I think we just hit the jackpot, Harrison."

The first fish fired at the starboard target had missed but had traveled on and struck the lead ship in the convoy's port-side column. The ship listed heavily, smoking.

A searchlight glared across the length of the S-55.

"They've spotted us, sir."

Small arms fire crackled from a nearby ship. A machine gun rattled.

Charlie gulped. "They're directing aimed fire at us."

"Helm, swing to northeast."

The S-55 turned, slow, too slow, as falling rounds stitched the water around them. The air buzzed with flying metal. Tracers popped as the machine gun zeroed in.

Figures lined the rails. Dozens of flashes of small arms fire.

Charlie flinched as it registered they were shooting at *him*.

He swallowed hard and said, "He's a troopship."

The troop transport began to cross Frankie's bow. The S-55 glided past floating bodies and pieces of burning wreckage. Men tread water, screaming.

Charlie looked down at them in horror, helpless to do anything to save them from the destruction he'd taken part in.

"Harrison! Eyes forward!"

He tore his eyes away and focused on the deadly landscape. The first target was gone now, swallowed by the sea. The second was sinking fast with a grating sound of chewing metal. With the exception of the troopship, the other ships were scattering and still firing wildly.

A series of heart-stopping detonations rocked the night as the third target exploded.

"Holy shit," Fredericks said from the shears.

A bullet ricocheted off the deck gun. Another thudded into the metal sail. A third cracked by Charlie's ear. Too close.

He gasped, "Sir, it's getting pretty hot up here."

"Wait for it," Kane said.

"Reload completed on number two tube," Reynolds said. "Reload completed forward."

"Fire one!"

"Firing one!"

Charlie said, "The fish has gone erratic, sir." Then he caught sight of the rear escort coming fast with a bone in his teeth. "Destroyer, bearing oh-seven-five relative, 2,000 yards!"

In seconds, the ship would fire a salvo from his bow gun.

Tracers streaked between two of the fleeing merchant ships and the incoming destroyer weaving between them. In the confusion, the panicking sailors were firing at their own escort.

The destroyers bow gun roared. The shell punched the water near the S-55 and exploded.

"Fire two!" Kane roared. "Clear the bridge! Take her down!"

The lookouts spilled down the trunk as the boat began to slide back into the water. She went under in sixty seconds, leaving behind a swirl of foam.

"Left full rudder! Come to south by east! Balls to the wall!"

The first depth charge explosions rattled the boat, but they sounded far abeam on the port side. The boat tilted steeply as she plunged into the depths. The officers nodded to each other, the only celebrating they had time to do.

"Passing eighty feet," Rusty said. "Fathometer reading, 130 feet."

"Very well. Rig for depth charge."

Another explosion. Seconds later, another.

Marsh gripped his headphones. "Two hits on target, now astern. Screws stopped. He's sinking fast, Captain."

That was the troopship. Charlie grinned at the captain. They'd hit four ships! Even the erratic torpedo had somehow found its target.

Kane winked at him. "Sometimes, you get lucky."

Charlie shook his head in wonder. The man wasn't

kidding.

"Passing 100 feet," Rusty said.

They heard distant thunder as the Japanese ships broke apart during their tumble to the bottom. Steel plates tore and buckled as the sea crushed them in her embrace. Then another boom and shake. Charlie guessed the troopship's boiler had gone up.

More crashing depth charges, but far away. When the lead ship in the port-side column had been hit, the destroyer's skipper must have believed two submarines were attacking the convoy. He was now attacking a ghost contact. Sometimes you got *very* lucky.

Charlie's elation turned to nausea. They'd just killed a lot of people. Hundreds, possibly thousands—that troopship had been packed with soldiers and had gone down fast. His mind flashed to tiny flaming figures tumbling into the foam. Men screaming in the oily water.

The stress of the attack caught up to him and turned his legs to jelly. He gripped the jammed periscope for support.

"Final trim, 150 feet," Rusty reported. "Fathometer reading, ninety."

"Ships, bearing one-eight-oh, 1,500 yards," Marsh called. "Fast screws."

The escorts were coming hard and fast. Charlie looked at Rusty, who stared back at him blankly, his face pale. He pictured his friend saying, *It's all fun and games until somebody gets hit in the face with a depth charge.* But for once, Rusty's humor had reached its limit.

"Helm, come to south-southeast," the captain said.

"They're speeding up," the soundman said. "They're coming right at us."

Charlie toughened his nerve. The game was still in progress. Frankie's achievement wasn't just a story; it was legend. Now he had to survive to tell it.

BATTLE OF BLANCHE BAY, OCTOBER 21, 1942.

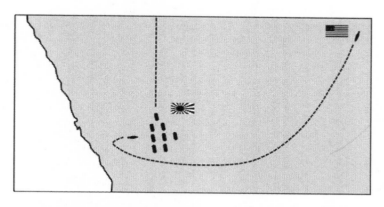

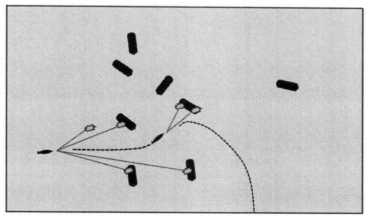

CHAPTER TWENTY-FIVE

CHARLIE'S TRICK

By now, Kane should have rigged the boat for silent running and taken his chances on straight flight, but he hadn't given the order. He had something else in mind.

"Reduce speed to one-third," he said.

Frankie had drained much of her battery power during the approach and flight. She'd need the rest to escape. She'd scored big in the IJN's backyard. The Japanese were out for blood.

The Japanese were notorious for abandoning a sub chase after a good thrashing, making survival a waiting game. This time would be different. Right now, Charlie knew, more destroyers were coming out of Rabaul to join the attack. Patrol boats and fighter planes.

This time, they intended to hunt the submarine until they destroyed it.

"Stand by to rig for silent running," Kane said.

Charlie studied the captain who'd just sunk four ships in a daring night surface attack. The man looked as drained as

Charlie felt.

He and his crew had just achieved a major victory in the war. It proved that when it came to a boat's battle effectiveness, the crew mattered most. Even with a broke-dick old boat like Frankie, men could still accomplish great things—with the right amount of luck.

Yes, the captain had pushed his luck to the edge. The Japanese hadn't detected the presence of an enemy submarine until the first torpedo hit them. The first fish shot at the starboard target had missed but hit another ship. The first three ships each sank after being struck by a single Mark 10 torpedo. One of the escorts pulled away to chase a ghost sonar contact. And the second escort had gotten caught up in the tangle and ended up being fired upon by his own ships.

In the end, though, the captain had made his own luck with skill and daring. Charlie regarded Kane's example as a submarine skipper's formula for success: temper aggression with reason and patience, and act decisively and tenaciously when the best move presented itself.

Rusty said, "You know what, Charlie? I think Lucy and Evie might be more proud than furious right now."

Charlie started in surprise as his brain experienced a sudden turn from combat to his personal life. The man was right. He'd thought of Evie as a woman who didn't understand war and, if she had her way, would hold him back from his duty. He'd been wrong.

Evie understood war. She'd cried when he'd told her he was going to the Pacific to fight in the submarines, but she'd supported his decision. She hadn't been selfish. He had.

She'd stood by him while he chased his dreams, knowing full well he'd be gone for a long time, possibly never to return.

He'd let a woman like that slip through his fingers.

"Rusty," he said. "I'm the biggest fool there is."

His friend smiled at him. "After we get through this, you can send that letter yourself."

It was a crazy conversation to have moments before a depth charging, but Charlie felt better having it. Talking about the future, and thinking about Evie, calmed him a little.

The captain said, "Now let's see if that trick of yours works, Harrison. Manifold, put a bubble in the number one main ballast tank but leave the vent open."

"Aye, aye, Captain."

The manifoldman adjusted the valve. High-pressure air shot into the tank and vented into the surrounding sea.

The air pocket floated to the surface and popped.

The last time they'd been depth charged, the vent being left open had been an oversight, and the large bubble bursting on the surface had marked their position. Charlie remembered that and had suggested doing it intentionally — to lure the Japanese where they wanted them.

"Rig for silent running," Kane ordered. "Helm, right full rudder. All ahead full."

The fans cut out. The planes went into manual operation. The planesmen pulled on the wheels to keep the boat on an even keel, the muscles bulging along their arms and backs.

Just ten minutes of such hard work was enough to drain a

man's energy. Two hands stood ready to take over once they'd exhausted themselves.

Short-scale pinging filled the boat. The destroyers were closing in.

"All compartments rigged for silent running," the telephone talker whispered.

The boat shuddered. Booms in the water.

"Depth charges astern," Marsh said.

The Japanese had taken the bait, attacking the area the S-55 had just vacated.

"Steady as she goes," Kane said.

The thrashing of the enemy screws became louder.

"Ship, 100 yards and closing," the soundman reported. "He's got us on sonar."

The captain frowned. "Ah, hell."

whoosh whoosh whoosh whoosh

"Splashes," Marsh reported.

The decoy had failed.

The men looked up, waiting. Seconds passed.

WHAAAMMM

WHAAAMMM

WHAAAMMM

The men hung on as the explosions shook the boat. A light bulb shattered. Dust drifted from the bulkheads.

Close, but not too close. The depth charging stopped.

The destroyer's screws speeded up as it made another run at its invisible foe.

whoosh whoosh whoosh whoosh

WHAAAMMM

WHAAAMMM

click-WHAAAMMM

The close-aboard concussion struck the S-55's hull like a giant hammer.

Everything flared white. Charlie had a vision of fire roaring through the control room, consuming everything in its path.

Then it was gone, and he was hanging on for dear life as the shock of more concussions violently shook the boat and everything in it.

"Left full rudder!" Kane cried. "All ahead, emergency!"

Charlie heard a second set of screws churn the water overhead. Smelling blood, the other destroyer had joined the attack. Short-scale pinging.

ping

The sonar emitted a sound pulse and listened for its echoes. If the sound struck Frankie's metal hull, it would reflect back to the receiver and give away their position.

ping

Rusty looked up and whispered, "That sound. I really, really hate that sound."

ping

The pinging grew louder. It began to increase in frequency.

ping ... ping ... ping ... ping-ping ... ping-ping

"Helm, right full rudder," Kane said.

"Right full rudder, aye, Captain," the helmsman answered.

The screws speeded up overhead. The next ping

reverberated through the boat, ringing it like a gong. Creating a bulls-eye.

PING-PING

"They've got us now," Rusty said.

"Splashes!" Marsh hissed.

Above them, large drums full of explosives tumbled through the water.

The men tensed and waited for the next hammer to drop.

click-WHAAAMMM

click-WHAAAMMM

The impact hurled Charlie against the plotting table and then to the floor. A wrench flew through the air and shattered a gauge. Glass rained on him from broken bulbs, followed by a light spray of water. He couldn't breathe. Trimmed heavy and with the pumps turned off, the S-55 began to tilt with her bow higher than her stern.

She was sinking.

WHAAAMMM

WHAAAMMM

He struggled to his feet, fighting for air. His bruised diaphragm finally allowed a deep breath. He coughed on the dust that swirled crazily in the red light.

He caught sight of Rusty huddled with his back against the corner, gripping the machinery at his sides, his eyes clenched shut as he mumbled something.

He was praying.

ping ... ping ... ping

Thrashing overhead.

"Captain," Charlie gasped. "Captain!"

"Any other bright ideas, Harrison?"

"The next time a charge goes off close aboard, release another bubble. A really big one."

The captain glowered at him, more sad than angry. Then he nodded. "Torpedo room, load tube one with garbage and stand by."

Kane had not only adopted his suggestion but was taking it even further.

"Tube one ready, Captain," the telephone talker said.

"Very well. Manifold, stand by to put a big bubble in the number one tank, and leave the—"

WHAAAMMM

WHAAAMMM

"Vent open—!"

click-WHAAAMMM

"Now, Tomkins!" the captain roared in the quake. "Do it!"

"Aye, aye!"

"Fire one!"

The bubble from the ballast tank shot to the surface as a geyser. A flurry of trash, fired from the torpedo tube, reached the surface moments later and spread across the water.

"All stop," the captain said.

The screws stopped. The boat began to slow. The planesmen grunted at the wheels, fighting to maintain trim as she hove-to.

The decoy had failed.

Now they were playing dead.

CHAPTER TWENTY-SIX

POSSUM

ping .... *ping* .... *ping*

The S-55 hung dead in the water, completely silent.

Taking water and trimmed heavy, she was slowly sinking.

Charlie's ears rang, deafeningly loud, in the aftermath of the explosions. Dust had gotten into his lungs. He had to cough, but he held it back. The longer he waited, the worse it got.

Rusty waved at the captain. He made his trembling hand level and slowly lowered it. He held up one finger, then nine, and then circled his index finger and thumb to make a zero.

Their depth was 190 feet, and they were still sinking.

The hull groaned loudly under the pressure.

Charlie looked at the creaking bulkheads. Frankie's scarred old pressure hull was the only thing preventing them all from being crushed by the vast amount of water surrounding them.

Even after a hellish depth charging, that was a sobering fact. At 190 feet, water pressure reached 5.75 atmospheres, exerting a force of eighty-five pounds per square inch. The boat had been tested to ninety pounds, but that had been back when she was in prime condition.

The seconds ticked. The boat drifted down. The captain signaled the planesmen to put full rise on the planes. As the S-55 became heavier, she began to tilt even farther. The men held on as the slippery deck angled sharply under their feet.

ping .... ping .... pi—

The enemy sonar cut out. The thrash of their screws faded into the distance.

Through the haze of red dust, Charlie saw the captain turn toward Marsh. The soundman held up two fingers and waved. The two destroyers were leaving. He raised one hand, as if about to make a karate chop, and then angled it. Northwest. Back to Rabaul.

The ruse had worked. The battle was over. Charlie leaned against the plotting table. He couldn't stop shaking. During the depth charging, he'd been calm and able to think clearly. He'd suppressed all the horror and stress, but now the fight was over, it caught up to him.

By now, the urge to cough was so strong, he felt like he was asphyxiating.

"All compartments, secure from battle stations," the captain said.

Charlie coughed explosively, took a deep breath, and coughed again.

"Secure from depth charge. Secure from silent running. Get those pumps working. Report leaks." The captain heard no response and wheeled. "Grimes?"

The telephone talker nodded dumbly at his station. "Okay," he said. "Yeah." He stared at the sound-powered phone hanging around his neck, as if unsure why it was there.

"Belay that order. Grimes, report to your berth and get some rest. Chief, see that he gets there. Reynolds, relay the order personally, and get me a replacement to man his station."

"Aye, aye."

"Motor room," the captain said. "Engage the motors. All ahead one-third."

The motors cranked the propellers. The boat accelerated through the water. With the aid of speed, she began to level out and gain some buoyancy, though she was still heavy.

"Helm, all ahead full," the captain said. "Manifold, blow emergency." Then he shot a smile at Reynolds.

Reynolds returned it. "Payback's a bitch."

"Marsh, any ships on the move up there?" The captain frowned. "Marsh?"

The soundman didn't look so well either. He shook his head. "No contacts, Captain."

"Very well. Planes, take us up to forty-five feet."

Damage reports poured into the control room. A long list of electrical failures, mechanical breakdowns, and seawater leaks. Another hatch gasket blown in the engine room. Forward compartments had no lighting. The main gyrocompass was out of action, as was the electrical steering. The engine exhaust valve leaked. The starboard engine air compressor was dying.

Rusty slowly pulled himself up to his feet. "I'll start organizing the repairs, Captain."

"Very well. I'll get an auxiliaryman on this broke-dick scope so we can see what the hell is up there." He looked at the clock, which had shattered. He rubbed the face of his wristwatch and brought it close to his eye in the dim red light. "It's 0130. We've got five hours of darkness to get it done, so let's get on it. Harrison, when we surface, you'll take first watch."

"Aye, aye, sir."

"In the meantime, I want you to—"

"Splice the mainbrace, aye, Captain," Rusty said. "Come on, Charlie. I'll go with you. I'm going to need a belt before I deal with this disaster."

Brownish water spilled into the control room from the aft passageway, bringing with it strong odors of brine and oil. The current, thick with struggling cockroaches and bits of trash, flowed over their feet. When the watertight engine room door opened after the captain declared, "Secure from depth charge," the water had poured out of the room in a rush.

Charlie gaped at the alarming amount of water.

"We'd better get to the surface fast," Rusty said, "or we ain't getting there."

Charlie and Rusty entered the aft passageway and stood aside as an auxiliaryman splashed past with his tools to fix the jammed periscope.

They proceeded a little farther and stopped. Rusty swept the area with his flashlight. "Swell. Just swell. Look at this mess."

The staterooms had collapsed, the wreckage piled in several inches of brackish water. The shock of the blasts had broken the pins that held up the wood frames and walls. The lockers had blown out; their uniforms and personal possessions had been flung across the room. Cockroaches scuttled up the walls to escape the deluge. Gibbon's *Decline and Fall of the Roman Empire* had somehow gotten stuck to the corking on the bulkhead, presiding over the mess like Ozymandias.

"The captain's right," Rusty said. "Fuck this fucking boat."

"Looks like we'll be sleeping in the conning tower for a while," Charlie said. His eyes widened. "Check that out. There, look."

"It can't be. Are you kidding me?"

They picked their way through the wreckage. Rusty stumbled with a curse. He shined his flashlight on a bulge in the bulkhead. Shorn of corking, the dull metal glinted in the light beam.

"I'll be damned," the engineering officer said. He ran his hand gently along the dent. "Gives you some respect for the amount of force unleashed by those bombs, doesn't it?"

Charlie gulped. It was a miracle they were still alive. "It gives me a little more respect for Frankie, that's for sure."

"I take back what I said, Frankie," Rusty said. "You're a tough old broad. Okay, Charlie, let's go get that drink. This calls for a toast that we're actually somehow still breathing."

The boat surfaced. All night, the auxiliarymen feverishly

attacked the repairs while a bucket brigade wearily bailed water out of the boat and the pumps worked overtime to empty the overloaded bilges. Charlie handed out the depth charge medicine, stood watch, and spent the rest of the night and morning doing the tedious work of splicing wire and rewinding the starboard motor. One of the mains topped up the battery while the other propelled the boat down the channel that separated the islands of New Britain and New Ireland.

By morning, the boat still needed a lot of work, but she could dive. She did so after the lookouts spotted a plane bearing down from the north. The battery powered the electric motors, which engaged the propellers. The S-55 made way at three knots until she reached the Solomon Sea.

They were still deep in enemy territory, but the way home was open sea now.

CHAPTER TWENTY-SEVEN
THE BLOODHOUND

Charlie patrolled the boat during his two-hour, below-the-deck first dog watch. He listened for dripping water. He smelled for smoke and any odors beyond the usual diesel stink. He felt the air currents for proper ventilation. He made sure valves were secured or open as needed, bilges dry, and trim tank gauges within the acceptable range.

His conclusion: Nothing worked properly anymore on this battered old boat, but it worked.

"Just a little farther, old girl," he said. "We're going home."

He passed the crowded mess room and paused to watch the men devour their suppers. They'd worked around the clock for three days to continue repairs to the ailing and cranky boat. Tonight, the weary men finally celebrated their victory. They dined on pork chops that tasted like freezer burn, the last of the fresh food. For the rest of the voyage, they'd be on iron rations, eating out of cans. Johnson played a Benny Goodman record over the loudspeakers. The men hummed along to "Jersey Bounce." The cook brought out a massive cake; he glowed as the crew cheered the sight of an iced S-55 sinking a troopship on top of it.

Morale soared. Tokyo Rose herself had singled them out as a plague and called them pirates, which made them feel like celebrities; sailors all over the South Pacific listened to Tokyo Rose's propaganda broadcasts. She'd also proudly confirmed that the S-55 had, in fact, been truly sunk this time, which prompted a big cheer from the men. Several chanted, "If Rosie says it, it must be true!" to much laughter across the room. It was a real celebration.

Charlie heard Braddock bragging to his friends that the boat would get a Presidential Unit Citation for the action at Blanche Bay. The machinist caught him looking and offered up another enigmatic wink.

Charlie barely noticed. A Presidential Unit Citation! Since the battle, he hadn't thought further ahead than getting back to Brisbane in one piece, but Braddock was right. There might be laurels at the end of this. Possibly even promotions. Certainly, Captain Kane, who before this patrol was looking at being taken out of the game, had put himself into a prime position to be given a new fleet boat. Admiral Lockwood needed fighting skippers, and he had one in Kane. Right now, the men would have followed him to the Sea of Japan.

The war would go on, might go on for years. Last night, Johnson picked up an ALNAV message, stating that the Japanese had landed a fresh division on Guadalcanal. They'd launched a ferocious assault against the ragged Marine entrenchments at Henderson Field. The Marines held on by a thread. The fate of Guadalcanal still hung in the balance.

The Japanese didn't give up easily. Like Rusty said, they really knew how to fight, and they were more than willing to die for their cause and their emperor. Yes, America needed fighting skippers to win this war. Charlie now knew he wanted to be one.

He arrived in the control room and gave his report to the captain, who stood next to Johnson on the sound gear.

"Very well," Kane said absentmindedly.

"Nessie, sir?" Charlie asked him.

"Nothing today. Maybe he's given up."

For the past two days, the sound gear detected the screws of a distant ship, but repeated looks through the periscope revealed nothing. The night watch observed a winking light in the distant dark, possibly a searchlight. The vexed captain had started calling the mystery contact the Loch Ness monster.

Yesterday, on periscope watch, Rusty detected a glimmer of masts and stacks of a ship on the northern horizon. Johnson heard long-range sonar pinging. The S-55 was being followed.

Today, nothing. Maybe the ship had lost Frankie's scent and gone somewhere else.

"Let's hope so," Charlie said. He wasn't sure Frankie was up to another fight. "I've been checking on the men. They're in high spirits, Captain."

"They should be proud."

The lights turned off. The control room rigged for red.

"Planes, forty-five feet," Kane said.

Darkness was falling, and it was time to surface for the night.

"Holding at forty-five feet," Reynolds said. "Our trim is good."

"Very well." The captain put on his sou'wester hat. "Up scope."

He scanned the surface while water splashed on him from the upper bearings. "Our luck is holding, gentlemen. The scope isn't fogged, and I can actually see." He shut the handles. "Down scope. Rig to surface."

Charlie hung his binoculars around his neck and confirmed his lookouts had arrived. For the next two hours, he'd be on the bridge for the second dog watch.

"Engine room, secure ventilation," Reynolds said. "All compartments, shut the bulkhead flappers." He turned to Kane. "Ready to surface in all respects, Captain."

"Very well. Surface."

The surfacing alarm sounded.

"Manifold, blow the main ballast tanks," Reynolds said.

Charlie climbed into the conning tower. Rusty sat up and rubbed the sleep out of his eyes.

"Can you guys keep it down?"

"Sorry, pal, we're getting set for the watch," Charlie told him. "Working Navy, here."

The boat tilted as she rose.

Rusty yawned. "I don't know what I'm going to do first when we get back to Brisbane. Sleep for a week or get drunk for a week. I'm thinking, get shit-faced until I forget all about this war. What do you think?"

"I think you should go with your gut."

"What's the first thing you're going to do?"

"Mail a letter."

The engineering officer laughed. "I said you were a go-getter."

"Twenty-three feet and holding," Reynolds said.

"Open the hatch," Kane ordered.

The quartermaster cracked the hatch and pushed it open. Fresh air began to enter the boat through the main induction.

Charlie mounted to the deck and scanned the night with his binoculars. Nothing but a flat, calm sea. "All clear! Lookouts to the bridge."

Fredericks, Peters, and Billy Ford emerged and took their stations.

The same old routine, repeated all day, day after day, on the boat. It had become as much a part of Charlie as the boat now was. He smelled smoke as the diesel engines fired up, one engaging the propellers while the other recharged the battery.

"I'll bet there were 2,000 soldiers on that troopship," Fredericks said.

"Hell, at least," Peters said.

"They won't be going to Guadalcanal and shooting any Marines, that's for sure."

"Speaking of shooting, one of those bullets came this close to my left ear. I heard the snap."

"Yeah, you told me. Like ten times."

"If I'd been wearing a hat, it'd still be floating around up there in Blanche Bay."

"If your head was any bigger, it'd be up there too."

Billy Ford added nothing to the exchange. Since he'd missed having a front row view of the battle, he'd fallen into a rare and sullen silence.

With a charged battery, the S-55 made full on both mains, cruising south across the Solomon Sea. Charlie thought about mailing his letters to Evie. He'd been wrong, though; that wasn't the first thing he'd do in Brisbane. The first thing he'd do was check to see if he'd gotten one from her. His stomach flipped at the possibility of seeing her feminine handwriting and what it might tell him.

The lookouts wouldn't shut up about the torpedo attack.

"The lead ship was an ammunition ship," Fredericks said. "That's why he exploded."

"You're talking about the starboard target?" Peters said. "I thought his boiler went up."

"No, he had a belly full of ammo. I'm sure of it. There were multiple explosions. The ship blew apart section by section. Didn't you see that?"

"Well, what happens when the boiler blows up?"

Charlie turned and said, "That's enough, gentlemen. Save it for—"

BOOM

The sea lit up with a blinding flash. A shell ripped through the air and punched the water a hundred yards off the port-side bow. The water exploded in white spray.

"Holy shit," Fredericks said. "What was that?"

A beam of light flickered across the water and fixed its glare on the S-55.

"Clear the bridge!" Charlie screamed. "Dive, dive, dive!"

Another flash in the darkness, revealing the bow of a Japanese destroyer. A second geyser erupted from the sea. Water splashed across the main deck.

The men poured down the hatch. The diving alarm honked as Frankie began her rapid slide back into the depths.

The naval gun fired again, a heavy boom that vibrated through the hull. Another splash.

"Destroyer, 4,000 yards," Charlie said breathlessly, still rattled by the suddenness of the attack. "He was just lying there, hove-to. Waiting for us."

"Planes, take her down," the captain said. He ran his hand through his shaggy hair. "Son of a bitch. That skipper must have spent the entire day circling around to come out ahead of us."

"Fast screws, bearing three-five-oh," Johnson said. "Turn count says twenty-six knots."

"Helm, left full rudder. All compartments rig for depth charge."

The destroyer began short-scale pinging.

"Nessie reveals herself at last," Rusty said.

"He's not an *Asashio* or *Fubuki*," Charlie said. "I don't know what class he is. He's one of the escorts from the convoy we attacked. I recognized him from his lengthened forecastle."

Reynolds looked at him sharply. "A long forecastle with a break forward of the bridge?"

"I think so. Yes."

The captain said, *"Minekaze* class." An old-timer, like Frankie. "What's she doing out here looking for us? The entire IJN thinks it sunk us back at Rabaul."

"The plane," Charlie said.

"Explain that."

"We were spotted while we were finishing up the repairs. Word got to the destroyer that he was tricked. He came back to finish the job."

The captain agreed with him. "So he's been pulling that routine for days. Search, circle around, wait. This time, he found us. We've got a very dedicated skipper up there."

"Yes, sir."

"Whoever he is, he's a bloodhound."

Reynolds had turned pale, his wide eyes fixed on nothing.

"Mizukaze," the man breathed.

Charlie tensed as the destroyer's screws chewed the water above them.

Of all the ships ...

whoosh whoosh whoosh whoosh

He flinched, expecting a good shaking, but there was no explosion. The tin can passed overhead without dropping any depth charges, sonar pinging steadily.

The screws receded to the west. The men looked at each other. What the hell?

"He's circling," Johnson said. "He's coming back."

The destroyer returned at high speed and did another dry run. Then another.

The message from the Japanese skipper was clear.

He wasn't going anywhere, and he was in control.

CHAPTER TWENTY-EIGHT

SLOW DEATH

Silent running.

Right full rudder, left full rudder. It didn't matter.

The little destroyer with its bloodhound skipper stayed on top of them, pinging steadily.

The captain ran his hand over his bearded jaw. "This might take a while." He looked puzzled. "That skipper is a hard case."

"He'll never give up," Reynolds said.

Kane squinted at him. "What makes you say that?"

"Because that's the ship that sunk the 56. I'm sure of it."

For the first time since Charlie had met the man, the captain paled with fear. "Jesus Christ."

Apparently, Kane was well acquainted with the exec's story.

But not his story anymore. All along, Reynolds had been hunting the *Mizukaze* alone on a personal crusade. Now the S-55, in turn, was being hunted. The fortunes of war had reunited Reynolds and his nemesis, and now the crew of the

S-55 had joined to his fate.

They were all in it together now. Charlie wondered with a shiver whether history was about to repeat itself. Or whether instead, perhaps, they'd help Reynolds get his revenge.

The destroyer's screws beat loudly over their heads as it made another run. This time, the ship dropped a single depth charge that pounded the hull. The men held on during the jolt.

A reminder of who was in charge. An invitation to come up and play.

"We've still got two fish left," Charlie said.

Reynolds snapped out of his funk. "That's right. We can take him."

The captain shook his head. "Not yet. We'll bunker down and shake him off."

The executive officer opened his mouth but closed it.

The S-55 slowed to a crawl. All lighting and instrumentation was turned off. The helm and planes were already on manual operation for silent running, and the pumps turned off. Men spread soda lime on the deck to absorb carbon dioxide from the air. All hands not needed for duty were ordered to their bunks to minimize noise and oxygen consumption.

Now came the waiting game. If the submarine stayed silent and down long enough, the destroyer might lose her or give up the hunt. If the destroyer stayed on top of the sub, eventually Frankie would run out of power and air. She'd have to surface and fight an uneven battle.

They waited. On the surface, dawn broke. Japanese planes

would join the hunt. The dark and quiet control room took on a funereal atmosphere.

"Harrison, Rusty, go get some rest," the captain said.

They went to the wardroom to play cards instead. Charlie brushed the cockroaches off the table as Rusty dealt hands for a game of Go Fish.

"I don't get it," Charlie whispered. "That Jap skipper definitely knows his business. What's he doing on an old *Minekaze* instead of, say, an *Asashio*?"

Rusty shrugged. "Maybe he's a little go-getter like you, bucking for promotion. Maybe he pissed off the wrong admiral."

"Got any fives?"

"Go fish, buddy."

Charlie drew a card from the deck. "Have you ever been in this situation before?"

"Sure, but we always got out of it. If we stay down and stay quiet long enough, he'll probably lose track of us and give up. If he doesn't, well ... then I guess I get to say, 'I told you so.'"

"We'll have to fight him. Take our shot with the torpedoes and the deck gun against his four big naval guns."

"He's got torpedoes too, and his probably work. We've got one advantage. The ship has a design weakness. The amidships guns have limited sighting. The ship's superstructure gets in the way. If we keep our bow aimed at him broadside just so, he'll have a hard time hitting us."

Broadside, a destroyer made a big target. In contrast, a submarine lay low in the water with a small profile. With her bow pointed, she made an even smaller target.

"We can do it," Charlie said.

"There you go again."

"It's possible," he protested.

Rusty laid down a book of aces. "Got any tens, Superman?"

Charlie handed them over.

Rusty said, "Fighting a destroyer on the surface is more like cards than chess. You start the game like chess, and then it's all luck of the draw with bad odds."

They played for hours as the boat's air slowly fouled. Charlie went to get them coffee, but the coffeemaker had been turned off along with everything else.

They decided to turn in and try to sleep. They climbed into the conning tower and sacked out with splitting headaches. Charlie tossed and turned. The boat was quiet except for the loud, grating pings that continually yanked him from the edge of slumber.

Men were screaming in Japanese. He didn't understand the words, but the language of terror was universal. He saw flaming figures topple off the gunwales of a burning ship.

Charlie awoke breathing hard in a pool of his own sweat.

ping ... ping ... ping

He glared at the bulkhead. That goddamn sound. It was like psychological warfare. He shined a flashlight on his watch. He'd been asleep for a record eight hours. They'd been under for twenty-four.

Rusty still slept, breathing in short little gasps.

Their air was dying, slowly being consumed one breath at

a time.

The conning tower's walls began to close in. He felt like he was in a coffin. He sat on his mattress and hugged his ribs, rocking, saying, "Shhh, shhh, shhh."

The last thing he or the crew of the besieged boat needed was for him to have a claustrophobic panic attack.

He told himself to get a grip. This wasn't about him and his bullshit, he reminded himself harshly. Everybody's life was on the line here. This was life and death.

He took as much air into his lungs as he could and let it out in a sigh. He stood, feeling dizzy from fatigue and heat, and descended into the control room. The boat had become impossibly hot; the thermometer read 130 degrees. Water condensed on the bulkheads and trickled in rivulets. The planesmen grunted at their wheels, sweat pouring off their ridged muscles, skivvy shirts tied around their heads like pirate sailors.

"Captain and the exec are in the wardroom," the quartermaster told him and gave him a handful of salt pills. "Better take these, Mr. Harrison."

"Thanks, Jakes."

Nine hours of sweating had depleted Charlie's body of much-needed salt. He hoped the pills would revitalize him, but he had a feeling they wouldn't. His ass and groin itched and stung abominably; he had the prickly heat bad.

His sandals splashed in a quarter inch of slimy water as he plodded toward the wardroom. He found Kane and Reynolds stripped down to skivvy shorts. A plate of stale sandwiches lay untouched between them. He poured himself a glass of tepid water and gulped it down with the salt pills. He looked at the captain.

"He's still up there," Kane said. "We almost lost him in the night, but he found us again at daybreak."

"How much time do we have?" Charlie asked him.

"We can last the day, maybe. I've been bleeding oxygen from the emergency tanks, but it's not enough. We're down to twelve percent of air composition."

Earth's atmosphere was twenty-one percent oxygen.

Charlie sat, picked up a sandwich, and put it back on the plate. Kane returned to his solitaire game. Reynolds took out a cigarette and put it between his lips, breathing rapidly through his nose. When he rubbed a match against the box's striking surface, the flame died instantly. Not even enough oxygen to produce fire. He flung the moist cigarette on the table.

The exec rubbed his forehead. "We can take him, Captain."

"I know how bad you want to sink that ship, Reynolds. We're not there yet."

"The battery's dying. The planesmen can barely keep the boat balanced at this speed. The crew is dropping from the heat. Our bilges are filled to the danger zone. We're sinking and starting to tilt."

"We still have time. This skipper's good, but nobody's that good. We'll lose him."

He was right, Charlie realized. Nobody was that good.

He remembered the smoke trail beckoning him toward the Q-ship.

Submarines didn't produce smoke while submerged. What would a boat leave behind that could mark a trail?

He excused himself and walked slowly out of the room. He found Braddock in his bunk, lying with his arm draped over his eyes. Every other bunk had a man in it either sleeping or staring into space in a dull stupor.

"Braddock, you awake?

"I could be."

"I need you to help me with a leak."

"Just take out your dick and aim it at the bowl, sir," the machinist said.

"An oil leak, Braddock."

The burly man opened his eyes and propped himself up on an elbow. "Where?"

"That's what I'm trying to find out."

Charlie believed Frankie was leaking oil into the sea. A steady stream of black bubbles rose to the surface and marked their position. That's how the Japanese skipper tracked them. Frankie had been leading the destroyer to her with a trail of black breadcrumbs.

Braddock stared at him. "Are you going to move aside, sir, or should I fix it from here?"

In the engine room, the machinist got to work. Charlie slumped against the bulkhead and listened to men wearily bailing water out of the motor room to keep the motors and gear dry. Everybody seemed to have their finger in a dike on this boat.

A grimy mist hung in the air. His ass itched and stung. He had a raging headache.

"God damn it," he hissed.

Braddock found a hole in a lube oil line and repaired it. "That should do her, sir."

"Outstanding," Charlie said, feeling hopeful.

Braddock growled, "Yeah, and don't tell anybody I did that so quick, or they'll double my work load. I do enough of the shit work around here."

The auxiliaryman plodded back to his bunk. Charlie shook his head as he watched him disappear into the dark passageway. The boat's biggest jerk had likely saved them all again.

He returned to the wardroom. Rusty was eating one of the sandwiches. Kane plowed through his solitaire game. Reynolds had finally gotten a cigarette lit.

The captain smiled after Charlie finished his report. "Now we can finally shake off this joker. We just need to hang on a few more hours."

"Good work," Rusty said, but he was frowning. As engineering officer, he should have thought of the possibility of an oil leak. They all should have. But with so much stress and so little oxygen on the boat, nobody was thinking clearly.

"John Braddock deserves the credit," Charlie said. "You should see how fast he works."

He noticed the pinging had stopped. A good sign. The screws began to recede.

The S-55 crawled along. The officers moved to the control room and waited. And waited.

At last, Kane ordered, "Planes, forty-five feet."

The planesmen groaned at the wheels, laboriously taking Frankie up to periscope depth.

"Up scope." He clapped the handles back into place. "And once again, I can't see anything. Down scope. Up number two scope."

Kane stared into the eyepiece for a long time while water from the bearings splashed across his shoulders.

Charlie couldn't stand the suspense. "See anything, Captain?"

"Well, Harrison, the scope is half fogged and vibrating, it's overcast and dusk up there, and it's raining on me inside my own boat. Give me a minute, will you?"

Charlie shut up.

A minute passed. Kane said, "We'll have to risk it. Stand by to surface."

A fresh pair of men arrived to man the planes.

"Surface." As the surfacing alarm sounded, he said, "I'll go up and take a look myself. Lookouts to the control room. Harrison, once I give the all-clear, you'll take first watch."

"Aye, aye, Captain."

Kane ascended the conning tower, Charlie following. As the boat broke the surface, the quartermaster removed the dogs and cracked the hatch. What sounded like a gale vented explosively through the gap. The hatch opened. The captain climbed out.

And came back down fast. "Dive, dive, dive!"

The boat shook as the *Mizukaze* fired a salvo.

The planesmen hauled at the wheels to angle the boat back into the sea while the manifoldmen flooded the ballast tanks with seawater.

Kane descended to the control room gasping. He stood for several moments leaning with his hands on his knees, struggling to breathe.

"Maybe he is ... just that good. What's he doing now, Marsh?"

"Just sitting there. Wait. Now the ship is heading toward us, slowly."

"Planes, 100 feet. Helm, right full rudder."

The men sagged. The destroyer was still on top of them, the battery was close to flatlining, and the boat was almost out of oxygen. They were out of options, and they knew it.

Reynolds stared expectantly at the captain. "Sir?"

"That Jap skipper wants a fight." Kane rose to full height and glared at his officers. "And we'll give him one. When it gets nice and dark, we're going to sink the bastard."

CHAPTER TWENTY-NINE
GUN ACTION

The sun set over the Solomon Sea. Twilight turned to darkness. The moon had not yet risen. The officers stood in the control room, waiting for the order.

The room was bathed in a dim red glow. Charlie glanced at the other officers' faces. He saw more than fear in their eyes. He saw a fierce will to fight.

An animal never fights so hard as when it's cornered. When it has nothing to lose.

"I think a Hail Mary is in order," Captain Kane said.

The officers smiled. He smiled back at them. He looked proud.

He could have given a rousing speech. If he ever wanted to get sentimental, now was the time. He looked like he wanted to, but he didn't. He probably knew there was no need.

"I'll be on the bridge. Harrison, as gunnery officer, you'll be with me to spot for the deck gun. Reynolds, you'll be assistant approach officer as normal. Rusty, assistant diving officer."

"Aye, aye, Captain," they said.

"We're going to fight. We're not going to surrender. That's it."

"Aye, aye."

"Torpedo room, make ready the tubes. Order of tubes is one, two. Set the depth at four feet."

"Tubes one and two ready to fire, Captain," Reynolds said.

"Rig for collision. Stand by to surface."

"All compartments report rigged for collision. The boat is ready to surface in all respects."

"Very well." The captain closed his eyes in concentration. Charlie knew he was looking for a better move, but he had none. He opened his eyes and said, "Battle stations, gun action."

The general alarm honked through the boat. The quartermaster repeated the order over the loudspeakers. Charlie descended to unlock the padlock for the ammunition locker. The gun crew assembled in their bulky steel helmets and stacked cartridges in the passageway. Sailors formed a human chain leading to the gun hatch, ready to pass shells up the line.

Charlie strapped on his own life jacket and helmet before leading the gun crew up to the main access trunk. The quartermaster waited at the top, gripping his mallet.

"Ready, Butch?" Charlie asked the gun captain.

"We're ready, sir."

"We drilled for this repeatedly," he told the gun crew.

"Make every shot count, and keep it hot."

They grinned back at him like wolves, panting on the boat's dying oxygen. Even the surly Braddock appeared to relish the prospect of a fight, however uneven.

Only Billy Ford showed his anxiety. Then he smiled to hide it. Charlie smiled back.

"Surface," Kane said.

High-pressure air pounded into the ballast tanks. The S-55 had to get to the surface fast and with an even keel, which would allow the men to get to the gun quickly.

The captain climbed into the conning tower and gripped the top rungs of the ladder.

Charlie reported, "Gunnery officer ready, Captain."

"Target is small destroyer, bearing one-six-five, range 4,000 yards. Good luck, Harrison."

"You too, sir."

"Planes on zero," Rusty ordered.

"Harrison," a voice said from the bottom of the ladder. "*Charlie.*"

He looked down and was surprised to see Reynolds looking up at him with a fierce expression.

"Sir?"

"I want you to sink that fucking tin can for me. Put him on the bottom where he belongs."

"Wilco, sir."

The gun crew cracked grins at Reynolds's language. Profanity was a fine art practiced regularly by enlisted men and rarely by officers.

"Promise me, Charlie."

"That's a promise, sir."

The water outside the portholes foamed. Frankie blew clear. The men tensed.

"Twenty-three feet and holding," Rusty said.

Kane said, "Stand by for battle surface. Open the hatch, Jakes."

The quartermaster hammered it open and threw it wide. The men craned their necks toward fresh air. The captain climbed out.

"God be with you men," Jakes told them.

Charlie hissed, "Gun crew on deck! Go, go, go!"

The men followed him up into the night. Charlie watched them rush down the steps to set up the four-inch deck gun. He took a moment to drink a deep lungful of cool, sweet, clean oxygen. The black sky appeared vast and limitless overhead.

Additional crews emerged from the hatch with fifty-caliber machine guns, followed by the lookouts, who took up their posts.

The gun hatch opened. The sailors passed up shells to the gun crew. Braddock rammed the first shell into the breech and slammed the block shut—again, Charlie noted with a scowl, neglecting to set the safety. The pointer elevated the seventeen-foot-long barrel for a 4,000-yard shot. The trainer rotated the turret. The sight setter made a slight correction. Butch gave Charlie the thumbs up. Ready to fire.

The Japanese skipper had been expecting them. A bright searchlight swept the water.

The boat's diesel engines fired.

The light swiveled and glared at the S-55.

Charlie cried, "Commence firing!"

"Fire!" Butch bawled.

The gun roared with a flash of light. The shell ripped the air and struck the water astern of the destroyer. Borkowski caught the hot empty case that ejected from the smoking breech.

"Check fire!"

Charlie called out the range and location of the miss relative to the target. The sight setter corrected the angle and elevation.

Braddock rammed the next shell into the breech and slammed it shut. "Ready!"

"Fire!"

The next round splashed fifty yards off the beam.

"Check fire!"

"Ready!"

The *Mizukaze* fired its bow gun. The shell tore into the sea a hundred yards astern and exploded. A hill of water rose above the impact.

"Fire!"

The deck gun roared again, missing the destroyer off the bow. The gunners had straddled the target. They had the ship zeroed. The next shot had a fair chance of hitting.

"He's turning toward us," Charlie said.

The captain stared at the ship through his binoculars. "All back full."

"Fire!"

The shell hit the destroyer amidships with a flash and

boom that sent bodies and shards of metal cartwheeling high into the air.

The gun crew whooped.

"Silence!" Charlie roared. "Resume firing!"

"I believe we struck the bridge or close to it," Kane said.

"Ready!"

"Fire!"

The destroyer didn't complete its turn but instead kept its heading, momentarily disoriented. Then the ship turned sharply, its bow gun pounding another hill out of the sea close aboard. Shrapnel clattered and bonged against the pressure hull. One of the lookouts screamed and plummeted to the main deck.

"Damn," Kane said, looking down as sailors rushed out of the stern access hatch to carry the wounded man below. He returned his gaze to the *Mizukaze*. "Here he comes."

The destroyer advanced while the submarine retreated, but the destroyer was faster. The distance between the two vessels rapidly diminished.

The captain said, "Stand by, torpedo room." He added, "Harrison, I'm going to fire our last two fish down his throat. If he evades, I'll turn the other way. If he goes to starboard, we'll go to our starboard. Rake him amidships. Then we'll make a run for it."

"Aye, aye," Charlie said. He shouted orders to Butch, who gave him a thumbs up.

"Fire one!" the captain said. "Fire two! All ahead full!"

The torpedoes swished out of their tubes toward the oncoming destroyer.

The *Mizukaze* turned hard to port to evade.

Charlie spotted the wake of incoming torpedoes.

"Torpedoes, close aboard!"

"Left full rudder!"

The S-55 turned just in time as the enemy torpedoes streaked past. Too close.

Charlie shuddered. "Butch, adjust your fire!"

"Meet her," Kane told the helmsman. "Steady on this course. Watch your rudder!"

Holding steady, the S-55 crossed the destroyer's beam at 1,500 yards.

"Resume firing!" Charlie shouted.

"Fire!"

The boat's deck gun and fifty-cal machine guns raked the destroyer's starboard side. Tracers flashed between the close-aboard vessels. Rounds snapped through the air and thudded into the sail's metal skin.

The starboard naval gun pounded with a blinding flash. A mountain of water roared high into the air, obscuring Charlie's view of the *Mizukaze*. The spray rained across the bridge.

"Reduce elevation!" Charlie waved at Butch. "Hit him below the waterline!"

One good hit below the waterline, and they could sink the bastard.

Butch gave him a thumbs up as his body disintegrated and pitched back into the water in a stream of tracer rounds. Borkowski flopped onto the deck, decapitated. The 20mm rounds thudded into the deck before punching Billy Ford through the chest.

Where the gun crew had been, only two survivors cowered on a deck splattered with blood and entrails.

Charlie gaped in horror. Then he shoved it aside. He'd feel it later, if there was a later. "Our gun crew has casualties, Captain. I'm going down there."

"Very well," the captain said. "Left full rudder! All ahead, emergency!"

The boat was running.

Charlie raced down the steps to the deck gun. A mutilated figure scarcely recognizable as human occupied the chewed up and smoking pointer's seat. He pulled the body onto the deck with an anguished cry. He wheeled on the survivors.

"On your feet! Man this gun!"

Tate lay on the deck with his arms covering his head. "Are you *out of your fucking mind*?"

John Braddock stood up, streaked with blood. "We're dead if we do and dead if we don't. Hand me that shell, Lieutenant."

Charlie accepted a shell from the wide-eyed sailor in the hatchway, made sure it was set to ARMED, and handed it over. "Here!"

Braddock rammed the shell home. "Ready!"

There was nothing to fire at. The destroyer was behind them now, turning back in pursuit of its fleeing prey. Charlie needed to get more men on the gun during the breather.

He called to the captain, "Ready to resume fire when we see a target, sir!"

Kane said, "Very well!"

Charlie flew through the air as a deafening explosion hammered the boat. He came to on the main deck by the bow, his helmet gone, his hair almost in the bow wake.

The conning tower was on fire, pumping smoke into the sky.

"Captain!" he screamed. He coughed on broken ribs.

The boat had decelerated and was turning to port, out of control. Had the explosion wiped out the control room? Reynolds, Rusty, and the rest? Was anybody left?

He tried to stand, fell down. He felt an overwhelming urge to sleep and let somebody else sort out this mess. Instead, he grit his teeth and forced himself onto his feet. He limped, swaying drunkenly, back toward the gun.

"You've got nine lives," Braddock said. The machinist looked relieved to see him. "Tate was thrown overboard when we got hit." Braddock held out his hand to steady him. "You all right?"

Charlie didn't answer. He was watching the destroyer, parts of it afire and smoking, emerge from the darkness at full speed.

"Jesus," he breathed.

"Fuck me," Braddock said.

The ship was coming right at them.

The Japanese skipper was going to ram the boat.

"Down!" the machinist roared and tackled him to the deck. Charlie howled as the destroyer's prow crashed into the boat at the stern.

The world filled with the agonized shriek of metal as the *Mizukaze* rode up and over Frankie's hull. The ship listed and righted itself. The boat tilted under the weight, her bow in the air. Water sprayed around the destroyer's damaged bow. The vessels groaned as they settled, their screws stopped.

Braddock looked down at Charlie. "Now what? Lieutenant!"

Charlie grimaced at the pain in his ribs and struggled to breathe. He pressed his hand against his side. It felt warm and slippery with blood. "Now," he managed to get out, "we sink him."

The machinist grinned again. "Aye, aye."

"If we can get a shot, we'll put a round into him below the waterline."

An alarm sounded in the boat. More than a score of submariners shouted as they poured out of the gun hatch with rifles and pistols. Petty officers, chiefs, sailors, auxiliarymen, and messmates. Charlie saw the quartermaster and even the cook and Nimuel, the steward, emerge with weapons.

Reynolds appeared in their midst and racked a round into his Thompson submachine gun. Charlie's chest flooded with relief. A senior officer was still alive.

The exec roared, "We're taking that fucking ship! Who's with me?"

The men cheered and surged down the deck toward the destroyer.

What the hell was he doing?

It was madness.

Another Hail Mary, but they had a chance. Maybe, just maybe, it could work. This time, Reynolds was bringing guns to the gunfight.

The men scaled the *Mizukaze*'s chewed-up hull with ropes and grappling hooks. Figures raced along the deck, shouting in Japanese. Gunfire popped and flashed as men fired at each other at point blank range. Two sailors pitched into the water, still fighting as they fell.

Get out of there. Get the hell off that ship!

He knew Reynolds. The man wasn't going anywhere.

"Get me a shell," he said. "Get as many shells as you can find."

Braddock disappeared down the hatch and returned with two shells, which he laid gently on the bloodstained deck.

Reynolds and his boarding party had cleared the bow and advanced steadily down the slanted forecastle, firing as they moved. He wasn't going to stop until he'd killed the Japanese skipper with his own hands.

The exec surged ahead. "Come on, men!"

The submariners cheered and ran after him.

A distant blood-curdling howl: "*Banzai!*"

Scores of voices took up the shout: "*BANZAI!*"

White-uniformed sailors swarmed out of the superstructure and charged up the deck with bayonets fixed. A dozen fell to aimed fire. Then another. The rest kept coming through the smoky haze, screaming as they closed.

The submariners ran, turning singly or in small groups to fire.

Reynolds stayed behind. He drained his tommy gun with a primal roar and tossed it to the deck. He pulled his .45 and shot a sailor in the face as the man rushed him with a battle cry. He shot another and then another as they came at him howling.

The sailors closed and speared him through the chest. Even then, he kept fighting. Another sailor charged in and sent him flying over the gunwale. Charlie watched helplessly as the man plummeted through empty air. He struck the water and disappeared.

The Japanese sailors kept going, pausing only to bayonet the wounded. One by one, the submariners stopped to make a stand and were overrun. The survivors reached the gunwale and jumped into the sea.

A man barked commands. Sailors began to set up a machine gun. Rifles strapped to their backs, others gripped the ropes and swung themselves over the side.

Having repelled a boarding, the Japanese were now going to board the S-55 and take her.

Braddock had the gun aimed at the destroyer below the waterline. "Ready!"

"Belay that!" Charlie ordered. He pointed. "There! Elevate the gun!" They sat in the gun's opposite seats, Charlie rotating while the auxiliaryman elevated.

"Ready!" Braddock said.

The machine gun opened fire with a metallic bark. He saw the rounds chew the deck in a straight line leading up to the gun.

Charlie screamed: "Fire!"

The gun discharged with a blinding white flash. The shell struck the destroyer just below the gunwale. The machine gun disappeared in the fireball. A dozen bodies crashed onto

Frankie's deck. The two locked vessels shivered at the impact and settled again with a cascade of metallic groans. Smoke shrouded the destroyer's bow.

Charlie cranked the wheel to turn the gun. "Reload!"

Braddock hopped out of his seat and slammed a shell into the breech. "Ready! That's the last one! The other one's gone. The concussion tossed it."

"Did you set it to ARMED so we don't shoot a dud?"

"I'm not stupid, Lieu-fucking-tenant."

"It's our last shot. It has to count, you asshole. Reduce elevation."

"The waterline this time?"

"No," Charlie said. He pointed at the destroyer's stern, which lay angled within view.

"Are you nuts?"

"We have to be sure he sinks."

The man stared at him. Then he nodded. "Aye, aye, and amen."

They lined up the shot. Charlie got out of the seat and stood behind Braddock, checking to make sure the optical sighting was good. It was.

This is for Kane. For Rusty and Reynolds. For all of them.

"FIRE!"

Braddock stomped the firing pedal. The gun blasted its last round at the destroyer's stern.

The shell struck the neat stack of red-painted depth charges.

The world went white. Charlie again flew bouncing across the deck as the *Mizukaze*'s stern disappeared in a searing explosion.

Thunder. Heat and light. Tumbling and pain.

Charlie propped himself up on one elbow. His vision swam. Through a bright haze, he saw smoking chunks of metal plunge into the sea around the sinking destroyer. The Japanese warship shrieked as it slid off the submarine. Frankie shuddered and screamed as her nemesis left her embrace.

The *Mizukaze* sank in a massive wave of spray.

"Braddock!" he cried. "Braddock! Anybody! Help me!"

Charlie sank back as the shock passed and his numb body began to register piercing agony. He shivered on the cold wet deck, his mouth open in a soundless scream.

When the darkness came, he welcomed it with relief.

This is it, was his final thought.

I love you. I'm sorry. Be —

CHAPTER THIRTY

BURIAL AT SEA

"How many men did you lose in the action?" the skipper asked.

"Too many, sir," Rusty said. "Thirty-nine, to be exact. Another eight wounded."

The S-55 lay hove-to next to the S-57, fifty miles from Cairns. The S-57's skipper had come aboard and whistled at the damage. The mangled and charred sail covered with a tarp to keep the rain out. The grooves and gashes on the main deck, scored like giant talon marks. Bullet holes everywhere. Silent machines. A sheet of oily black water covering the deck.

In the wardroom, Captain Reyes, the S-57's commander, heard the story of how the S-55 sank five Japanese ships and barely survived the encounter.

The man shook his head in wonder. "A hell of a thing." He looked like he'd wished he'd been there but was glad he hadn't. "How did you get here without being able to dive?"

Rusty nodded to Charlie, who sat slumped in his chair. Charlie's left arm, fractured in two places, hung in a sling. He breathed with difficulty, his chest tightly wrapped against three broken ribs. Bandaging covered multiple gashes in his left side, which Rusty had treated with sulfa and hydrogen peroxide and taped shut until a doctor could treat him.

Charlie would be going home with scars after all.

"We set a fire in the conning tower," Charlie explained. "Blew fans at the smoke. Played with our trim. Pumped our bilges to create an oil slick. The two Jap planes that overflew us thought we were afire and sinking. They left us alone long enough for us to reach the Coral Sea."

"With one working engine and a leaking boat."

"We've got a terrific engineering officer sitting right here. We've also got a good machinist who kept us going. John Braddock. You can have him if you want."

Reyes shook his head again. "A hell of a thing. Perth was trying to reach you for days. We thought you were lost." He looked at Charlie. "This was your first war patrol, wasn't it?"

"Yes, sir, it was."

"Welcome to the submarines, Harrison."

Charlie smiled at that.

"Well." The skipper stood and put on his hat. "We don't want to be on the surface any longer than we have to in broad daylight. We can talk further on the 57 after you've rested. We've got your wounded aboard. Bring the rest of your crew over, and we'll scuttle the boat."

Charlie and Rusty exchanged a glance. Rusty said, "We're not coming over, Captain. We're staying with Frankie. We're going to deliver her to Cairns."

Reyes frowned. "The boat's a write-off. It's a crazy—"

"We fought for this boat," Charlie said fiercely. "Our crew bled for this boat. Our captain and exec died for this boat. This boat sank five Jap ships, and *we're taking her home.*"

The skipper sighed. "Have it your way. We'll cover you as best we can." He spread his hands. He didn't have to explain the risk they were taking. They knew it well.

They shook hands. Soon, the S-57 sank out of sight.

Charlie gazed across the calm, sunny water. The S-55 began smoking as she made way. He looked up at the metal sail and said a silent prayer for Captain Kane.

You never think a conversation you have with someone will be your last. Charlie remembered the last thing the captain said to him during their chess game.

Next time, I'll know exactly what to —

What was he going to say? Nothing important, probably. If Kane had known how close he was to his mortality, he likely would have said something very different. But as the last personal thing he'd said to Charlie, it took on great significance to him. A cryptic message Charlie could puzzle over for years.

No, that wasn't right. The last personal thing he'd said was, *Good luck, Harrison.*

Thank you, sir.

If Charlie had known it was to be their final exchange outside of combat, he would have said something different too. He would have spoken up and said how much he admired the man.

Kane's memory would live on in Charlie, and so would his tactics.

Goodbye, Captain Kane. Goodbye, Lieutenant Reynolds.

Both men, along with so many others, now buried at sea.

He walked along the deck and found Rusty on his hands and knees, leaning over the side of the boat with a bucket of white paint next to him.

The last commander of the S-55 finished painting a fifth meatball on the chipped hull.

"I'll find a broom," Rusty said. "The shears are gone, but we'll jury rig something to tie it to. Frankie's earned it. Five kills and a clean sweep. Our girl is going home in style."

"I guess that means we'll be on another boat soon. I hope they keep us together."

Rusty stared out over the water. "I don't want to think about that right now. I just want to get home." He growled, "While you were knocked out, I trolled the wreckage for survivors. The Japs were in horrible shape. Their clothes had been blown off. They were covered in oil. I tried to take a few prisoners, but every time we reached down to pull one aboard, he swallowed water and went under. They'd rather drown themselves than surrender. Who are these people, Charlie? How long is this going to go on? We got our five meatballs, but what did it cost us?"

Rusty didn't ask the last question left hanging in the air: Is it worth it?

As officers, they knew victory demanded a steep price. Charlie believed it was worth the cost but couldn't say exactly why. So he said nothing.

Frankie limped toward Cairns on one main engine. The next morning, Rusty made landfall. Cairns was a sight for very sore eyes. As the boat approached the harbor with a broom tied to a pole, the S-57 blew clear of the sea bow first and began to pace her as escort.

"Look at that," Rusty said with a grin. "Going home in style."

As they neared the harbor, Charlie frowned. Something was wrong.

The water level was rising.

"Goddamn, Frankie," Rusty said, close to tears. "Don't do this now."

Braddock ran onto the deck with the other four men of the skeleton crew who'd volunteered to remain aboard and get her home. Rusty looked at him. The man shook his head.

"She's taking water fast," Braddock told him. "We're going down. She's done."

"What do you mean, 'she's done'? How bad is the leak?"

"Leaks," Braddock corrected. "Water's gushing into the boat."

The heavy water in the boat was overwhelming the pumps and weighing Frankie down. The screws stopped as the water drowned the engine. The pumps died. The sea stirred around the boat. The deck tilted as she began to sink by the stern in a shooting spout of water.

She was going down fast.

Charlie said, "It's okay, Rusty. I think she knows what she's doing."

Rusty took a deep breath and let it go. The boat was obviously lost; there was nothing more to do here. "All right. Abandon ship."

The machinist grinned at Charlie. "Remind you of a certain special night, Lieutenant?"

"Shove it up your ass, Braddock," Charlie replied and then groaned as the man helped him into his Mae West life jacket. He wasn't looking forward to getting into the saltwater with his wounds.

"I'll help you swim over to the 57, sir. I won't let you commit *hara-kiri* just yet."

Charlie looked around at the old boat one last time and said goodbye.

A hell of a way to fight a war.

Rusty said, "That's it, gents. Over the side quick so we don't get caught in the suction."

They jumped in and swam away as Frankie sank gracefully into the spray. A burial at sea. The old sea wolf's war was over. She was calling it quits.

CHAPTER THIRTY-ONE

THE BEACH

Charles Lockwood was rear admiral and commander of the submarine force in the Southwest Pacific Theater. He welcomed the two young naval officers into his office in Brisbane.

"I just got off the phone with the new boss, Bull Halsey," the admiral said. "A phone call in which I was able to describe an outstanding patrol that resulted in five confirmed sinkings. The admiral is very pleased. The newspapers are going crazy over it back home."

"Thank you, sir," Rusty and Charlie said.

Evie knew he served on the S-55. Charlie hoped she was proud of him, and not too furious.

"There will be laurels for you and other distinguished personnel," the admiral said. "I'm recommending a Presidential Unit Citation for the boat and the Medal of Honor for both Lieutenant-Commander Kane and Lieutenant Reynolds. Their loss is a real tragedy."

They thanked him again, more heartily this time.

"The failed Jap offensive at Henderson Field was their last big try to take it back," Lockwood went on. "By Christmas, we'll have Guadalcanal wrapped up. Then we'll be on offense. We need fighting men in the boats, gentlemen. Men who will follow Kane's aggressive style. It's going to be a whole new ball game in '43."

"Yes, sir."

"Lieutenant Grady, the manner in which you rallied the crew and restored operation of the S-55 after the battle was exemplary. You've proven yourself ready to take on responsibilities of executive officer. You're to report to PXO school at New London."

"Thank you, sir," Rusty stammered. After a month of training at prospective executive officer school, he would enter the XO placement pool. If he performed well, he might command his own boat one day. He dazedly returned the man's handshake.

"Kane set the standard, son. I want you to sink ships."

"Understood, sir."

Lockwood turned to Charlie. "As for the man who sank the *Mizukaze*, I'm promoting you to the rank of lieutenant and posting you to *Sabertooth*. We need men who've got balls and can think on their feet. I see a promising career ahead of you if you stick with the submarines, son."

Charlie reeled at the heady news but kept his cool. He accepted the man's handshake while barely being aware of it. "Thank you, sir."

"You can thank me by sinking every one of those sons of bitches. Your squadron commander will fill you in on the details."

Charlie couldn't believe it. Just five weeks ago, he'd been standing on the wharf, eyeing Frankie's scarred metal sail with trepidation.

"I'd love to spend more time with you fine men, but there's a war on," the admiral said with a wry smile. "You've got two weeks of R&R before you report to your respective assignments. Enjoy it. Take a load off. Then you can get back into the fight."

Back outside, they walked along the path toward the wharfs.

"PXO!" Charlie exploded. "Congratulations, Rusty."

"You too."

Rusty said nothing for a while, apparently still dazed by their meeting with the admiral. For a blessed minute, Charlie forgot about the pain in his healing arm and ribs.

Rusty said, "I wonder if every guy who moves up the ladder feels this way."

"What way is that?"

"I'm wondering what the hell the Navy is thinking, for starters."

"Maybe we'll end up on the same boat again at some point."

"I'd like that, Charlie."

"In which case, I'll keep you on the straight path."

"Ah, go to hell. We'll both be faking it until we make it, and you know it."

Charlie laughed. He did know it.

He'd earned his combat patrol badge and his dolphins

marking him as qualified in submarines. His wounds had earned him a Purple Heart. His squadron commander told him he'd been recommended to receive a Silver Star for sinking the *Mizukaze*.

Even so, he still had a lot to learn.

The men walked along the sunny beach, hands in their pockets, each lost in his own thoughts.

At last, Rusty parked his rear on the sand. "I have no idea what I'm going to do now."

Charlie joined him on the warm sand. "I thought you wanted to get drunk."

"I have this urge to sit here for a while. Just sit here and be alive and know I'm alive. Look at the water without being afraid of it. It's peaceful here."

It was. They gazed across Brisbane River for a while. Charlie thought of home, San Francisco. A submarine glided into view. Going out to sea for a war patrol.

"Look at those poor fools," Rusty said. "Full of piss."

"Yeah," Charlie agreed coolly, but the sight made his blood quicken. He wondered who was commanding her, where she was going, and how she'd fare once she got there.

He wished the boat and her crew good luck and good hunting.

The submarine was one of the new fleet boats. *Gato* class. Three hundred feet long and twenty-seven feet wide at the beam, with a complement of six officers and fifty-four enlisted men. Four powerful diesel engines, four high-speed electric motors, two batteries. She could make twenty-one knots on the surface and nine knots submerged, up to 11,000 nautical miles and seventy-five days on patrol. She could dive to 300 feet. She carried twenty-four torpedoes. Her machinery was new. And she had air conditioning.

Sabertooth was a fleet boat. He was basically looking at his future command.

She was beautiful.

He stood and dusted sand off his service khakis.

"Where are you going?" Rusty said.

"To mail a letter. Come on. You probably got mail from home."

"No, I'll sit here a bit longer. I've got a lot to think about. You go. I'll catch up later."

Charlie looked at his friend and again saw a tired man grown old before his time, now facing the prospect of being an executive officer.

"Wait a sec," Rusty added. "Do you want the letter back that you gave me?"

"No. Keep it." Charlie patted his breast pocket. "And I'll keep yours. Until this is over."

After writing letters to Mrs. Kane and Mrs. Reynolds, he'd written a new letter to Evie. In it, he'd admitted his selfishness, his need for her, his gratitude that she'd both loved and supported him while he went off to fight his war and left her alone. He told her his love and memories had gotten him to hell and back.

Then he asked the question: Could she forgive him? Love him again?

If she said yes, he was going to marry that girl. If she said no, he was going to keep asking.

"I'll see you later then," Rusty told him. "We'll get into a bottle of something and celebrate."

"You got it." He added with a devious smile, "Exec."

"Oh, brother."

Charlie left his friend on the beach and headed to the post office.

By deciding to send his letter to Evie, his destiny awaited him there, just as it awaited him on his next command. He'd learned that destiny wasn't something you ever reached; it was a path. A path defined by choices, directed by strategy, and ultimately decided by the luck of the draw.

Charlie's war was just beginning, and so was his destiny. He welcomed its next chapter.

WANT MORE?

If you enjoyed *Crash Dive*, continue the adventure by reading the next book in the series, *Silent Running*. In this book, Charlie sets out on a rescue mission to the Philippines...

Learn more about Craig's writing at www.CraigDiLouie.com. Be sure to sign up for Craig's mailing list to stay up to date on new releases.

Turn the page to read the first chapter of *Silent Running*. After that, you'll find a special note about this book from the author.

CHAPTER ONE

REMEMBER PEARL HARBOR

Naval Station Pearl Harbor, Hawaii.

December, 1942.

Charlie Harrison set down his sea bag and smiled at his new home.

The *Tambor*-class submarine lay tied at the end of a pier that extended from the jetty housing the submarine base. A sea tender refitted her for war. Shirtless workers in dusty dungarees toiled in the sun amid a tangle of hoses, wiring, and gear.

Rivet guns whirred. Sparks flew from welds. Trucks unloaded spare parts. A pair of sailors in a rowboat repainted the hull. Mattresses hung on a line to air out. Charlie watched the sailors go through their routine.

No sign of the crew, who had long left for Oahu's beaches and beer halls.

The submarine lay a football field in length and twenty-seven feet wide at the beam. When on the surface, four massive GE motors drove her at a top speed of twenty knots. While submerged at depths as low as 250 feet, a pair of Sargo batteries propelled her up to nine knots. She could travel an impressive 11,000 nautical miles.

Her name was *Sabertooth*.

Like all submarines, she was named after a creature of the sea. The sabertooth fish was a small but fierce tropical predator with big curved teeth. *Sabertooth*'s teeth consisted of twenty-four torpedoes, which she fired from six tubes forward and four aft.

Lieutenant-Commander Robert Hunter captained the boat. With a name like that ... Charlie had hoped it was an omen, that the captain knew how to find and sink Japanese ships. Back in Brisbane, he found out *Sabertooth*'s war record spoke otherwise. Three patrols, only two sinkings.

To the west, dozens of powerful warships lay moored among calm blue waters and waving palm trees. Pearl was a militarized Eden. Then he spotted the distant listing hulk of the great battleship *Oklahoma*, still half-submerged in the water. A grim reminder of the day that started the war. December 7, 1941.

In just a few days, the Navy would mark the first anniversary of the vicious surprise attack.

Charlie couldn't stand here, where America's war began, without feeling reverence for the dead. That, and a sense of awe. He gazed across the harbor waters and tried to picture what it must have been like on that terrible day.

Two hundred fighters and bombers roared out of the rising sun.

He knew the story well enough; every man in the Navy knew it. Every fist-clenching, teeth-grinding, blood-boiling bit of it.

The first wave assaulted Battleship Row and the six airfields. In only minutes, a bomb crashed through the Arizona's *two armored* decks and struck the magazine. The resulting explosion ripped her sides open like tin foil and broke her back in a massive fireball. She sank within minutes, taking more than a thousand souls down with her.

Six torpedoes hammered the West Virginia, which also went under. Nine torpedoes drilled into the Oklahoma, making her list so heavily she almost capsized. The fighters strafed the airfields, chewing up the planes parked wingtip to wingtip in neat rows.

Then the second wave screamed out of the clouds; 170 planes joined the attack.

Flag flying and AA guns blazing, the Nevada steamed through black smoke toward the open sea. A swarm of howling bombers surrounded her. After several hits, she beached herself off Hospital Point.

For the men at Pearl, it had been two hours of pure horror.

Charlie could imagine it now. Bombs whistling. Geysers from misses. The great battleships bucking at the hits. Black smoke rolling across the sky. Planes roaring. Tracers streaming up from the AA guns. The bow of the destroyer Shaw exploding in a spectacular spray of fire and debris.

The men screaming in the water. The water afire and choked with corpses.

Everybody helpless against the merciless onslaught.

A year ago, he heard the news of the attack while serving on the destroyer Kennedy in the Atlantic. He'd listened to the President's address on the radio. He'd joined the submarines hoping to pay the Japanese back for what they did. He'd longed for action, and he'd found plenty of it on his first war patrol with the S-55. He had the wounds, Silver Star, and promotion to prove it.

Now he stood ready to do his duty and get back into the war.

The ghosts of this war still haunted Pearl, but so did the martial spirit of an angry, awakening giant. The battle had ended, but the war continued. A reckoning was coming. Japan had started it. Men like Charlie were determined to finish it.

For this was not a battle of nations, but of men, and of the endurance of men.

NOW AVAILABLE...

AFTERWORD

Thank you for reading *Crash Dive*! Welcome aboard!

Every story has influences and a beginning, and I thought I'd share mine here.

I'd read the entire beloved Hornblower series by C.S. Forester in about two months and was struck by what I consider a simple formula of "men, machines, action." Flesh-and-blood men made larger than life not just by their heroism, but by their flawed humanity. Machines, in Forester's case big wooden sailing ships, which themselves become beloved characters through an attention to detail that makes the reader feel like he or she is aboard. And action—gripping, bloody action. All of it served up with convincing realism.

Around that time, I was going to the library once a week to take out a nonfiction book and expand my horizons. On a whim, I picked up *War in the Boats* by Captain William Ruhe, who served on a variety of submarines during the Pacific War. Through his amazing stories, I finally figured out why boys love submarines, and I knew I had to write this novel. A novel that would portray a young lieutenant's first war patrol on an older S-class boat during the bloody Battle of Guadalcanal, welding a you-are-there "men, machines, action" story onto these historic events.

Crash Dive is influenced by Ruhe's extraordinary account of his experiences on the S-37 along with many other books written by and about submariners during World War II. When the war started, only about 50 submarines were in service; by the end of the war, some 180. Though hampered by older equipment and faulty torpedoes in the early days of the war, submarines sank more than 1,100 merchant ships with a tonnage of some 4.8 million by its end. They also sank about 200 warships, including eight carriers, a battleship, and 11 cruisers. Strangling Japan's economy and by extension its ability to fight made a major contribution to the American victory—a victory that seems inevitable today but was far from certain in 1942.

Japan's anti-submarine tactics and equipment were arguably poor compared to the war's other major combatants. Nonetheless, the Japanese sank more than 50 American submarines during the war, or about one in five boats. Nearly 3,500 submariners died in these actions—a casualty rate six times higher than the rest of the Navy—making service on a submarine far more dangerous than on a surface ship. The Japanese hated the submarines. They took few prisoners; some were executed, while others suffered in brutal "special treatment" camps.

From the American perspective, the men who served on the boats were heroes and, during the war, largely unsung heroes. The Silent Service valued secrecy to preserve operational security and effectiveness. In subsequent years, the silence around the boats of World War II lifted. Today, we're able to learn about what it was like in the boats, what they did, how they lived, how they triumphed, and how much they suffered. If you enjoyed this fictional submarine adventure, you might like the real thing even more. I recommend *War in the Boats* by Captain William J. Ruhe, *The War Below* by James Scott, *The Silent Service in World War II* edited by Edward Monroe-Jones and Michael Green, *Clear the Bridge!* by Rear Admiral Richard H. O'Kane, and *Submarine!* by Edward L. Beach. I also recommend, for sanitized but very interesting viewing, *The Silent Service*, a 1957-58 TV series narrated by Rear Admiral Thomas Dykers; many episodes have been uploaded to YouTube.

These firsthand accounts went a long way in informing the writing of this novel, along with a great deal of other research that included Navy manuals related to S-class submarine operation and submarine phraseology. Any errors and omissions, of course, are solely mine, and many are intentional—artistic license to tell a simple, coherent, and dramatic story.

Thank you for reading *Crash Dive*. I hope you enjoyed reading it as much as I did writing it. If you did, please review this novel and tell your friends about it. Stay tuned for new episodes in the series at www.CraigDiLouie.com (be sure to sign up for my mailing list). I also welcome any correspondence about my fiction at Read@CraigDiLouie.com.

Thanks again for reading my work. I hope you enjoyed the voyage.

—Craig DiLouie, April 2016

ABOUT THE AUTHOR

Craig DiLouie is an author of popular thriller, apocalyptic/horror, and sci-fi/fantasy fiction.

In hundreds of reviews, Craig's novels have been praised for their strong characters, action, and gritty realism. Each book promises an exciting experience with people you'll care about in a world that feels real.

These works have been nominated for major literary awards such as the Bram Stoker Award and Audie Award, translated into multiple languages, and optioned for film. He is a member of the Horror Writers Association, International Thriller Writers, and Imaginative Fiction Writers Association.

Learn more about Craig's writing at
www.CraigDiLouie.com.

59115946R00144

Made in the USA
Lexington, KY
23 December 2016